Shifter and Spice

A Clan Conroy Duology

EMMA ALISYN

emmaalisyn.com

CONTENTS

One Bearry Night

A Clan Conroy Novella

1

Rebekah rolled on her side and swiped the phone as a harpsichord alert went off- the most annoying ringtone she could find to help drag herself out of bed in the mornings. Reading the message, she sat up, eyes widening.

"What the hell? This is the third reschedule this week!"

Thumbs flying over the touchscreen, she replied- using somewhat politer language than that coming out of her mouth.

:*We are happy to accommodate schedule changes. Is there anything wrong my studio can help with? - R. Conroy.*:

Dad would be irritated. He'd wanted to book this guy for a holiday special, but the pre-production deadline was fast approaching. If they didn't get a greenlight soon, she'd be scrambling to put together her backup episode.

The reply chimed a moment later. :*No- C.C.*:

Rebekah clenched her teeth, sliding out of bed to head to the bathroom as she typed.

:*If we're going to have a Winter Solstice special, we need to get all the details finalized. How about I come to Tacoma this week?- R. Conroy*:

She put the phone down and brushed her teeth. Ha. Let him wiggle out of a face-to-face meeting. Rabid curiosity as to what he looked like aside, a face-to-face meeting would be ideal- would let her lay down the law of actual television production. The internet stuff he did was great, which was why he'd captured the interest of Liam Conroy, celebrity chef and owner of the highest-rated shifter-owned cooking channel in the States. But she was losing patience- which was saying something, when this industry required nothing but patience.

:*Thursday. Meet me at my studio.- C.C.*:

A MapQuest popped up in the texts, giving her directions to his location.

"Yeah, baby," Rebekah whooped.

An actual address. She now had an actual address and would get to see the inside of the studio where he produced his episodes and confections, a mix of baking and molecular gastronomy that had built him a solid following among cooking and food enthusiasts. The fact that he filmed each episode from the chest down so his face remained a mystery would make scoring him for the holiday special even more of a coup.

Liam Conroy and the Chemical Confectionist. The ratings would make sweet, sweet bank. She was planning on asking for a Solstice bonus.

Rebekah finished brushing her teeth and choosing her version of workwear- working for her Dad had perks, one being the lack of corporate attire requirement. She hadn't much grown out of her teenage uniform of cargos, fitted tanks and plaid. Materials, cut and colors were more sophisticated, and depending on where she was she covered her sleeve of tattoos with a blazer, but she pretty much looked the same. Hair a few shades darker than natural, pale eyes with a thick triple coat of mascara and clear gloss on her lips. When she did nail polish, it was purple or navy- maybe this Solstice she'd go red to match the festivities.

Her cell rang and she hit answer before checking the ID- no one but family would call this early in the morning.

"Yeah?"

"It's Grandmother, Rebekah. I thought we might have tea this morning."

Rebekah made a face at the phone, finishing off her ponytail and leaving the bathroom, rooting around for black Mary Janes. Those were the last words many a Bear had heard before being roped into one of Gwenafar's machinations. Being human didn't give her a pass- not when she was the adopted daughter of Gwenafar's eldest son.

"I don't know, Dad wanted me to-"

"I won't take up much of your time," the female interjected, voice the kind of smooth that warned she'd not tolerate a no.

Damnit. "Yeah, okay. Now?"

"Did you have something else to do this morning?"

Plenty, considering her Dad was also her boss and that the internet personality she was tasked with tracking down was playing least in sight. But dear grandma didn't consider either her son, or Rebekah's job, to be anything else but amusing distractions from Den business. And the only reason Grams could want to talk to Rebekah now, using that tone of voice, was because of Den business. Maybe even Clan level, though Rebekah sincerely hoped not.

"I'll meet you at the restaurant-"

"No, let's go to neutral territory, hmm? How about that cupcake shop you like? They open early to serve muffins and hot beverages. I recall you prefer sugar for breakfast."

Oh.... God. Neutral territory and a bribe of a completely inappropriate breakfast? Rebekah's heart rate spiked. Now she really *was* worried.

"I'll be there in twenty." Best to let the sword hovering over her neck fall swiftly. That way the pain would be over soon.

Gwenafar was already seated, peeling the wrapper off a vanilla cupcake topped with a swirl of pink icing, when Rebekah arrived. An open box sat in front of her, each of the remaining cupcakes unique and colorful.

"The fruit filled are absolutely delicious," the older female said. "Have you tried the new one? Blackberry lemon."

She shrugged, careful to temper the moodiness of her body language at the last second. Gwenafar Conroy didn't take no sass- not even from her Alpha son. "I like fruit. Let me grab coffee."

Rebekah approached the counter, ringing the bell. A moment later a harried looking young woman rushed out, covered in flour and the cafe's trademark green and pink apron, face slightly flushed.

"Hey, Brick, the usual?"

They'd gone to school together, though Amberley was from a different social circle. One of the not-quite-cool kids with a two-parent household and enough money for sports fees every season. Not the kind of kid the teenage Rebekah had had much use or like for, but Amberley had never been snotty so now that she owned a business, Rebekah was more than happy to patronize it.

"Yeah. Any new flavors this week?"

Amberley fiddled with the new espresso machine, muttering under her breath. Rebekah had never actually heard the woman swear, but it sounded like a few choice words were leaving the baker's mouth now.

"Is the new equipment acting up?"

"I want to kick it." She finally got it working and turned around, frustration in light gray eyes. Strands of her ashy brown hair escaped its long braid. "You won't believe how much I spent on it, but my mom convinced me the way to catch the morning traffic is to offer caffeine."

Amberley moved to the cupcake case, pulling out a cookie dough cupcake. Vanilla cake filled with cookie dough batter, topped with a generous swirl of icing and a small cookie. "I'm going to start doing scones soon, and breakfast wraps."

"Expansion is good. Hmm, maybe Dad will consider doing a hometown small business episode."

Amberley's eyes widened as she clutched the counter. "Oh, joy. Me would love you long time. Like free cupcakes for life."

Rebekah laughed, taking out her wallet. Amberley waved a hand. "Mrs. Conroy already bought a dozen cupcakes, no charge for this one."

Rebekah's lips pursed, though she smiled. "That's no way to run a business."

"You'll be back."

Amberley handed her the drink, two shots of espresso

5

with brewed coffee, almond milk and caramel syrup, and disappeared back into the kitchen with a final thanks.

"That girl keeps calling me Mrs. Conroy," Grams said. "I'm ambivalent about that. She is polite though. I wonder if she's married?"

"Stop matchmaking, Grams. I'm a little nervous. What's going on?"

Gwenafar's dark eyes flicked to Rebekah's face, an amused smile on her lips. Normally it was a good idea not to show a predator fear, but Rebekah preferred the pretense of meekness with the Den Elder- especially since she'd seen the size of the female's fangs when angry.

"The Mother's Council asked I speak to you."

Rebekah coughed on a piece of cupcake. Grams leaned forward and hit her on the back.

"The Council?" Rebekah said, eyes watering. "What do they want with me?"

"You're turning twenty-six this Winter Solstice."

Instinct warned Rebekah that this conversation was about to take a horrific turn. "Yeah? I was thinking of asking Aunt Norelle to do a fancy cake. It's been a while."

"That sounds nice. You aren't mated, Rebekah."

Oh, shit. There was only one reason a female Elder of the Mother's Council would be concerned with the status of a human woman.

"Grams..."

Gwenafar's eyes pinned her. She unwrapped a second cupcake, not taking her gaze from Rebekah's face. Bears could pack away a shit ton of carbs and not gain a pound. Rebekah was more or less blessed with a fast metabolism- and Liam and Meredith were healthy eaters anyway, so she could get away with a second cupcake as well. Especially since she knew she'd need the sugar.

"You were raised as one of our own."

"Well- I was sixteen when Meredith and Dad adopted me-"

"You understand our ways. You understand the grave circumstances we face. Your family."

Rebekah contained a wince. Her inner rebellious teenager whined. Didn't like Gwenafar layering on the beginning of a guilt trip, didn't want to be roped into doing something she didn't want to do. But the adult woman, and the adopted daughter who'd always craved family, security- who would do anything for the people who had taken her in as one of their own- began to slump into a resigned puddle of acceptance. 'Cause she knew where this was going.

"You want me to pick a mate," Rebekah said, cutting the verbal dancing. She preferred straight words.

"We would like you to take your place among us." Gwenafar reached out a hand, clasped Rebekah's limp fingers. "You're a strong woman, and an asset to the community. You know we need our gene pool expanded to avoid sterilization. Before our young males look outside the community, the Council prefers they choose from those humans among us who are already allies. It makes so much more sense."

Rebekah closed her eyes a moment, fingers flexing in Gwenafar's hold. "Damn, Grams. I wasn't planning on doing the whole mate and cubs thing- at least not this soon."

She opened her eyes to see a dark brow rise. Gwenafar's pale face was unlined, but the years had threaded her coffee brown hair with silver and she'd cut it shoulder length to manage better. The silver was so evenly spaced, so glossy, it was almost as if she'd had it done at a salon. The Bear certainly didn't look like a human's idea of a grandmother. But Bears aged differently and rarely looked old- even if they were.

"You're thirty in four years. I hardly think this qualifies as a rush to the altar." Gwenafar paused. "I have an offer for you. Not quite in the community, but I think a suitable match nonetheless."

"What?" Rebekah stared, a rush of anger tightening her jaw. "It's one thing to talk to me about it- but you went behind my back and actually arranged a mating?"

Gram's expression cooled. "The discussions are preliminary, but my initial reports are very positive. An older male- despite what I said, I really don't think any of the Conroy males would suit you, you need someone more worldly- with his own business, from a small but healthy Den."

"Did you tell Dad about this?"

Gwenafar paused. "When he returns from his trip-"

"Did you tell Dad?"

Her lips thinned. "I'm not required to consult a Den Alpha regarding matters that concern the Mother's Council. It's our responsibility to ensure the young ones are properly mating and producing healthy cubs. It's Liam's job to-" she waved a hand. "-keep the males entertained until it's time for them to settle down."

Rebekah snorted. A Den Alpha's job was a little more complicated than that, and she was certain a Clan Alpha's job would be even more complicated. Liam did a hell of a lot more than keep the male Bears in the Den out of mischief.

"I'm not ready for-"

"You owe us, Rebekah."

She shut her mouth, staring at the female she called grandmother. The mother of the male she called Dad. She didn't call Meredith Mom cause their relationship had always been more of an older sister type thing, especially when Rebekah was younger. Her relationship with Harvey, Meredith's father who'd been incarcerated for murder most of his daughter's childhood, was more complex. He'd saved her life once, but even all these years later, he wasn't that emotionally stable. She and Meredith maintained a careful, if cordial, communication with him. It helped that Liam was a Bear, and the Den Alpha.

"I-"

"Liam took you in. Raised you. The Den welcomed you as one of ours. We've protected you from your biological family, included you in our ceremonies and community."

"And you did all that expecting me to pay you back?"

Hard eyes didn't waver. "I will expect no less from my biological granddaughters when they are of age. You happen to be the eldest and therefore the one tasked with creating a good example of selfless, responsible conduct for a young female of reproductive age."

"I think I'm worth a little more than to be your broodmare."

Gwenafar snorted. "We are female. None of us is above providing our Clan with cubs. It is our first, and most important, responsibility. The burden and privilege of our gender." The Elder rose from her seat. "Well?"

"Damn, you want me to give you an answer now?"

"There's really only one answer you can give and still live with your conscience. And this is not an attempt to bully you- I know you."

Goddamnit. Rebekah picked up a third cupcake. "I'm not having a baby right away. And if I don't like him, I'm not-"

"Of course not." Gwenafar patted her cheek. "No one expects you to mate a male you don't like. If this one isn't suitable, we'll find you another. Unless you have a beau you haven't said anything about? No? Well, we'll do it the old-fashioned way then. It will be fun."

Fun.

2

Daamin heard his mother's ringtone over the noise of the club. Glancing at his sister as she handled a customer, he activated the discreet Bluetooth in his ear.

"Yes, Mother?"

"Your sister hasn't come home for dinner."

Asiane's eyes flickered toward him. She heard the controlled anxiety in the older female's voice as well.

"Asiane is at work, Mother."

"No, she isn't. I drove by the cafe and the nice human man with the orange hair told me she isn't even on schedule tonight. She's missing, Daamin. You must find her. What if the-"

"We are safe here, Mother." He had to cut off that line of thinking, and quickly. It would do the females of his Den no good to worry about enemies at every turn. He'd prepared the older girls as best he could- and Asiane was not defenseless. The younger girls he could only keep as close to their home and wrapped in the layers of security his company provided.

Five sisters, and he was the only son. The oldest of his mother's cubs and tasked with protecting his sisters from their enemies. He needed more help. He needed a mate.

"Mother, have the girls had dinner yet?"

His question distracted her for a moment. "Yes, Talia made dolmas and Faridah did a salad- an American salad. There is barely any green in it. Daamin, where are you? I'll have one of your males bring me and we can-"

"No, Mother." Asiane would have to tell mother about the club acquisition sooner or later. Mother couldn't keep thinking her eldest daughter worked in a coffee shop. "We need you home to take care of the girls and back up security if there is any trouble." A Mama Bear was a Mama Bear, after all, even if she had no formal martial arts training. She still has claws, and teeth.

A human male sitting at the bar eyed Daamin sideways. He hadn't bothered lowering his voice since he was speaking in the rolling, lilting vowels of his homeland. The man looked spooked- probably all the nonsense on television these days. Daamin bared his teeth in a smile and the man slid off his stool and left. Daamin tracked his movements, watching to make sure he wasn't headed towards security.

"You should speak English," Asiane said, wiping the counter. "The Arabic frightens them."

"They're stupid."

"They're scared."

"Who are you talking to, Daamin?" Mother asked. "And what is all that music I hear? Are you at a party?"

"I'm at a club, Mother. I'll bring Asiane home, don't worry."

"Is that Asiane I heard? At a club?" Daamin winced as high-pitched indignation permeated Mama's voice. "A club is no place for an unmated female."

"We're in America, Mother. The rules here are different."

"I won't have my daughter working at a bar." Worry fled, Mama Bear's voice deepening to a growl. "Put her on the phone."

"She's busy. We'll be home soon and we'll discuss it."

It would only be a matter of time before the issue came up anyway. He hadn't actively lied to his mother; he just hadn't volunteered any information. His sister didn't look worried, though. Which she wouldn't be, being nearly as dominant as himself. He sighed. When Asiane told her, he'd simply pick a seat in a small corner and stay out of the way of any flying debris. He might be dominant, but he was no fool. And only a fool would come between two hissy females.

Asiane snorted, black eyes glittering with a combination of mirth and derision. He agreed to a point, which was why he escorted her to her shifts at the club and assigned a guard on the days he couldn't sit through her shift with her.

Mother would probably be even more upset if she knew Asiane was the owner and not just the bartender. He assured Mother they'd be home soon and disconnected the call.

"Distract her with Winter Solstice celebrations," Asiane suggested. "She said she wanted to celebrate this year. Something about teaching the girls appreciation of the local customs."

Daamin shrugged. He didn't care one way or another, and since his work required he learn about the winter holiday celebrated by many shifters in this region as opposed to the human Christmas, he supposed he could appease Mama with a show of cooperation.

"The girls were upset I wouldn't let them wear pointed hats and drink champagne for Al-Hijra. I think they have enough local 'culture.'"

Asiane laughed. "You know Faridah and Talia want to go downtown for the American New Year? They think because they are eighteen they can be allowed out all over the city at night."

Asiane's disapproving glower was rather funny since at their age she'd been just as wild as the twins were turning out to be- and still was. She was his younger sister by only a few years, but his nerves felt the age difference.

"Maybe I'll let them go with an escort. Or else they'll just sneak out." He eyed Asiane. As a male, he approved. As a brother and protector of their tiny Den- he winced. The black leather was fetching, and certainly very modern, but if she went home dressed like that, it would give Mother a heart attack. All that... bosom. "You'll change before we go home, right?"

Asiane rolled her eyes. "Don't I always? She was going to find out sooner or later. Why don't you stop hovering over here like a bad movie bodyguard, and go find some human girl to nibble on for a few hours?"

"I'm a Bear, not a vampire."

"Vampires don't exist."

Daamin snorted, eyes scanning the crowd. He'd probably take her suggestion. It was a quiet evening, and he needed something to distract him from business. From the email waiting in his account, answering his request to the Pacific Northwest branch of the Mother's Council.

The email with the name of his arranged bride.

"Make me a drink," he told Asiane. "Use the shifter stuff, not that human swill."

She mixed him up something- he didn't know what it was and didn't care- and slid it toward him with sympathy in her face. And amusement. She knew he'd asked for a mate and had been both for and against the idea. And thought it was hilariously funny he was... nervous.

What male wouldn't be? When the negotiations concluded, he would meet a female he'd never known, formally mate her, and then bring her home to the critical gaze of his traditional, highly conservative and controlling mother. He'd told the Council to find him a female with spine- a dominant if they could. Shifter, or human, since cross-species matings were highly encouraged these days.

"When will you meet her?" Asiane asked.

"I haven't even opened her file yet."

He took a long drink of the alcohol, liquid fire tearing down his throat. They hadn't had such things in the country where his family had lived for generations. The home they'd fled because of civil war- both human and shifter. His old anger stirred, fangs pulsing with a need to rend something. Males at his home, demanding three of his sisters be given over to the Clan leader as mates for his males.

The fight had been brutal, their flight to America taxing on the younger girls. The only thing that saved them was he'd already had an escape plan in place, seeing the way the Clan males eyed his older sisters. Eyed Asiane, the most beautiful and strong-willed of them all. She'd bear an Alpha strong cubs- but she was his sister, and he'd die before he allowed any male to mate her against her will. When they'd started making formal inquiries of the twins, not yet out of secondary school... Daamin had known it was time to go. His bloodline had dwindled, too many allies now dead or moved away. Even the strongest Bear couldn't fight an entire hoard of mate-hungry males on his own.

"Daamin."

He looked up.

Asiane leaned towards him, brow furrowed. "You cool?" She'd switched to English, her accent nonexistent.

"I'm fine."

"Good. Go skulk somewhere else, you're scaring my customers away. If I see something sweet, I'll send her your way. But no sex in my office."

He blinked, offended. Did she think so little of his virtue? Of course, he wouldn't take a female in his sister's office.

Asiane rolled her eyes. "It was a joke, Daamin. Stick, meet mud. Now go."

***

Rebekah entered the club, the bouncer waving her inside after a sniff. She'd paid a half rate because she was a girl and been handed a short list of rules. Basically, the look but don't touch the shifters kind of rules. She gathered it was a shifter seeker kind of place- where non-humans got in free because they were the main attraction. The humans were probably the main paying customers.

Weaving through the late after-work crowd, Rebekah glanced around. Because she'd mostly grown up in restaurants, and because it was her job to notice lighting and set, she appreciated the sophisticated decor. Modern, black with touches of purple. Exposed ceilings and an entire feature wall of multi-colored rough stone. The seating was also ultra-modern and durable.

She approached the bar, waiting until the bartender approached.

"What's your poison?" the female asked, a husky voice with the faintest trace of an accent.

Long, dark hair and bright dark eyes, the kind of perfect skin and contained energy Rebekah was used to seeing at home.

"You got any of the shifter stuff?"

The female's eyes sharpened, giving Rebekah a thorough look. "You smell human. And you don't look like a shifter seeker."

What the bartender meant was Rebekah was mostly dressed, and not already trolling for a free drink. Her arms were bare despite the chill in the early winter air, showing off her sleeve of tattoos, and her jeans were dark and tight. But other than that, she hadn't bothered with any of the usual female accoutrements. A real shifter male? They didn't like makeup. The scent and taste of it was revolting, or so she'd been told plenty of times.

"That's 'cause I'm not, honey."

The bartender leaned an arm against the counter, cocking a hip as if Rebekah were interesting. "This really isn't a place you come to enjoy the scenery."

The devil made her do it. "From where I'm sitting, the scenery looks just fine."

The female blinked, then grinned, a slow saucy smile. "If I was pan, I'd be tempted, *honey*. So, you want some of the real stuff, huh?"

"My Dad always let me have a sip at Solstice in the eggnog, but now that I'm a big girl..."

The bartender smiled. "Something to put hair on your chest coming up."

Rebekah turned, watching the crowd. The music reflected the age group of the clientele- patrons seemed to range from just out of grad school to early retirement age. Very few people were alone and most were in small groups.

"So," she said when her drink was placed at her elbow, "if I was interested in a night of adventure, how would you suggest I go about it?"

The female paused. "Just a night, no strings?"

Rebekah took a sip of the drink, let the burn loll around the inside of her mouth. The good stuff. "Yeah. A last hurrah before an arranged mating."

Dark eyes widened. "But you're human."

"Yeah. Adopted by a Den, though. The Mother's Council-" Rebekah paused. "You a Bear?"

It wasn't exactly a rude question, though it could be taken that way between strangers. The female didn't seem offended though.

"You've got a good eye." A slim hand reached out. "Asiane. This is my place."

Rebekah clasped the hand. "Rebekah. And it's a nice place you've got." She grinned. "So in that case, any recommendations? And I'm not talking about the drinks."

Asiane laughed, then paused, lips pursing. "As a matter of fact..."

The mirth in Asiane's face puzzled Rebekah, but she pointed through the crowd to a male. The male leaned against a wall, arms crossed, eyes scanning the crowd. A small circle of space around him, as if everyone knew he wasn't there to party.

"Is that security?"

Asiane snorted. "In a way. I happen to know he's available for the evening, and mostly sane. And not looking for a Claim, so you're safe in that regard."

Rebekah studied him. Tousled dark hair that needed a cut if he wasn't going for the rakish look. Deep set dark eyes and good bones- the shifter kind. Something about the curve of his jaw and mouth seemed familiar. Rebekah glanced at Asiane. Back at the male.

"Are you pimping your own brother?"

The Bear glanced at her, brow raised. "You *do* have a good eye. That's why I said 'mostly sane.'"

Rebekah smiled. It sounded like something her youngest sister would say about their brother.

"Go say hi," Asiane said. "Tell him dessert is on the house."

Rebekah swirled the remainder of her drink, amused. She supposed she was the dessert. But if the male wasn't an ass, and was as charming as the sister, she wouldn't mind being dessert.

Rebekah slid off her stool. "Okay, but if I break his heart, don't hunt me down."

She walked away as Asiane laughed. The male glanced over, probably alerted by the sound of his sister's amusement, and his eyes caught Rebekah's.

Smiling, she sauntered towards him, relaxed and ready to indulge herself. If the Council had their way, this time next month she would be mated.

God help her.

3

A female weaved through the crowd, the sway of her hips insouciant, occasionally flicking aside a hapless human with a subtle touch of a black-tipped claw. No- finger. Humans didn't have claws. This one looked like she should. If he didn't know better, he'd think her a cat of some kind, especially with the beginning of a self-satisfied smile curling her naked lips.

So. His sister had jokes.

"Asiane says I'm dessert," the female said when she was within earshot.

Interesting. No human would know he could hear, much less recognize that the statement was directed at him, unless the human understood shifter hearing. She didn't look like a seeker. The slope of her slender, pale shoulders was too relaxed. Her energy contained.

"You aren't normally the type she sends my way."

The female reached him, stopping a foot away. Her brow quirked, pale eyes intrigued rather than offended. Good. She had spine. It would make the evening more interesting.

"What's the normal type? An American blonde honey bee? Busty and dumb as a rock?"

"Are you saying all blondes are stupid? Or all busty women?"

She rolled her eyes and moved closer, leaning on the wall next to him, crossing her arms. Not in a defensive way, but for comfort.

"Of course not. I'd be a hypocrite to knock someone for their hair color."

Her long, straight hair was pulled back in a simple tail, and a shade too dark to be natural.

Reaching out a hand, he brushed a finger along her colorfully painted arm. "These are lovely."

She glanced down at herself. "Thanks. Still in progress. You got any ink?"

"No." It was forbidden among his people, technically. But he'd never come across an image he wanted branded on his body.

He looked closely at hers. "Is that a garden?"

She grinned, and Daamin saw one of her teeth was slightly crooked. "I met my Mother at an after-school gardening program when I was a teenager."

"Met your Mother?"

"I'm adopted."

She said it with no bitterness, only a quiet joy. What an odd conversation. "There's a story there," he said. And smiled, finally. She would do for the night. At least for the night. "Do you dance?"

She looked down at his feet. "Will you step on my

toes?"

"Only if you want me to."

***

This one was going to be fun.

Sometimes they weren't, but were pretty enough that she could ignore stupid for a few hours. Fortunately, Meredith had no particular hang-ups about sex, though she'd insisted Rebekah remain abstinent until she was at least eighteen. Since high school boys didn't even know how to wipe their asses properly, and who knew where they dipped their dicks, Rebekah hadn't had trouble following that stipulation. Once in college, she'd dated as often as she wished. Some years more than others, and in the last year less often due to a hectic work schedule. But work did something for her sex didn't- fulfilled an inner need. Sex was a physical itch, men a brief amusement. Work, helping Dad build his company, helping Meredith with the rambunctious cubs- those were the things that mattered.

Though now she supposed she'd be worrying about her own cubs.

Rebekah sighed. The male touched her cheek, drawing her attention.

"Problem?" he asked.

His voice was deep and smooth, the hint of an accent sexy. Dark eyes calm and thickly lashed. This was a male not ruled by his sexual energy, though it oozed plenty- because he let it. She glanced up at him and away, unintentionally coy. He'd unleashed just a hint of his sexuality in the spark of his eye and quirk of his mouth.

The brush of his finger against her cheek brief, but electric. Yeah, he knew what he was doing.

"No problem, just issues," she said. "But let's dance. I've got to put you through your paces, see what we're working with."

She captured his hand, emboldened enough by his permissive body language, and pulled him into the center of the club.

"I don't think you'll be disappointed, *habibti*."

Heat in his eyes, a croon in his voice. Strong hands slid lightly around her hips and he pulled her close- not too close, not taking liberties. A gentleman. She smiled, delighted. So many men just ignored the dance of consent, thinking a peek through the peephole meant the whole house was open, walk right in.

"I hope not, or I'll have to complain to management. And I'm pretty sure the owner likes me."

His brows shot up. The beat of the dance changed, something a bit slower but with enough of a punch she could move her hips.

"Should I be jealous of my own sister?"

"Nah. I only roll for poles."

He laughed. "Good. In a fight with Asiane, I'm certain who would win."

"You, of course."

He grinned at her dry tone. "Not at all. And not just because I can't bear to strike a female."

She moved in, just a bit, closing a small gap between their bodies. "So what's your name? Or should I make one up?"

"Daamin will do."

"Well, nice to meet you Daamin will do. I'm Rebekah."

"A lovely name- a bit common."

"Are you calling me common?"

"No- I just meant so many human females- ah... I think I'm going to rephrase my comment. The language difference, you know." And suddenly his accent was thick enough to be a winter blanket, while he blinked, eyes innocent.

She smiled. "Yeah."

Daamin took her hand, lifted it to his mouth and pressed a kiss on the back. The touch of his lips and gentle puff of warm breath shivered across her skin. Her torso tightened briefly. Damn. If he could do that just with a kiss on her hand... it had been- well, had she ever experienced this kind of chemistry? She couldn't recall.

"How are my paces?" He pulled her against him, executed a flawless turn and dip- completely inappropriate for the club and music playing, but laughter gurgled in her throat.

"Show off."

"For a beautiful female? Absolutely."

She glanced over his shoulder and saw Asiane leaning against the counter, grinning. The sister gave her a thumbs up.

"I'm not beautiful."

"Who told you that lie? Not your father, surely."

Rebekah's lips pursed. "Actually, he says I'm beautiful because I look like my mother- which is a bald-faced lie since we aren't biologically related."

"If he loves her, then it is not a lie."

"He adores her. They've been mated for ten years now."

"Mated?" He studied her face. "You're human."

He danced them towards the edge of the crowd. Rebekah noticed but said nothing. "Mom, too. But Dad is a Bear."

She shut her mouth on the fact that Dad was also an Alpha- she'd made the mistake a few times in her dating life. Shifter males tended to be wary of the daughter of an Alpha- the potential drama involved if Papa thought his little girl was being taken advantage of.

"Ah. I wondered if you knew what I was."

"An incredibly sexy man with a killer accent and bedroom eyes?"

They were outside the ring of lighting, partly nestled in a hall she knew should be off limits to anyone but staff. He pressed her back against a wall, gently, not disallowing escape should she so choose- but letting her know he was very interested in getting to know her better. Especially as his hips brushed against hers. A subtle tease, or a mistake? Looking into his eyes, she knew it was no mistake. He was in perfect control of his body.

His head lowered, mouth brushing her ear. "Tell me more about my eyes."

She inhaled as his head turned, mouth hovering over hers. Rebekah licked her bottom lip, throat suddenly dry. "Isn't that my line?"

"Whose line is it anyway?"

He muffled her startled laugh at the corny joke with a kiss, lips pressing against hers even as his body pressed her against the wall, arms on either side of her head.

Smooth lips, breath scented with whiskey and mint tea,

25

his touch a gentle demand for her response. She opened her mouth to him, tilting her head to give him better access. Her body began to pulse, heart beating quicker.

Rebekah's hands crept up to his shoulders, and he flexed under her touch. Her favorite part of a man- besides the obvious part- was his shoulders. Daamin's were well shaped, not too broad, but clearly sculpted with hard muscle, the kind from labor and genetics rather than an obnoxious number of hours at a gym. He deepened the kiss as her hands slid around his arms to wrap around his wrists. Imprisoning him as he imprisoned her.

He pulled away, voice husky. "More?"

She wasn't sure if his idea of more and hers were the same thing. "Yes, more. As much as you want."

His eyes captured hers. "Then be mine for the night."

"Show me."

Daamin pulled her down the hall, opening a door and stepping aside so she could enter a dark room. The sound of a click and the noise from the club was muffled. A light came on, bright at first and then dimmed to around twenty percent. A desk in the room, and a deep leather couch along one wall. Tall potted plants in the corner and a flat screen television on one wall. Probably to monitor security footage.

Rebekah turned. Daamin leaned against the door, arms folded, watching her. "The door isn't locked," he said. "You can leave any time you want. No matter how... deep my wants go."

It was just a one-night stand, an encounter between two strangers agreeing to share pleasure for an evening, provide solace without risk. But for a moment she wished it was more. How often did a girl meet a male who didn't think chivalry was dead?

"Okay," she said.

He approached, a new liquidity to his movements, a growing burn in his eyes as a smile played around his mouth. He was unleashing the Bear, just a little. Just enough. Rebekah inhaled, taking an involuntary step back.

"You can run if you want," he said. "I'd enjoy that."

"I'm sure you would." She arched a brow. "So you're the rough and tumble type."

He closed the space between them, chest brushing against hers as he lifted a lock of her hair, let the strands slide through his fingers.

"Maybe. If you want me to be. What am I allowed to do to you?"

Oh, shit. "That question has connotations. Do I need a safe word?"

He considered her, then shook his head. "No. Even willingly, I wouldn't go that far with a female I've only just met. We haven't had enough time to trust each other in that way. So… no rough and tumble. But sit on the couch for me. Spread your legs."

Rebekah backed up, dropping onto the couch when it bumped the back of her knees. He crouched, sliding her flats off her feet, running his hands up her inner thighs until he reached the waistband of her pants.

"I think you'd be more comfortable without all this cloth on," he said, a deep dark croon, and pulled the leggings from her body, leaving only her scrap of beige lace panties.

She swung her legs up on the couch and he adjusted, coming up over her. Rebekah wrapped her arms around his neck, opening her thighs to cradle him. When he kissed her again, in addition to the mint and alcohol she tasted hints of a cinnamon mint he must have snuck while she wasn't looking. Rebekah grinned against his lips. How cute. He hadn't wanted stinky breath.

Fangs nipped at her bottom lips, hands roving over her torso, underneath the drapy knit blouse she wore. He pushed it up to her chin, exposing her breasts, and unclasped the front of her bra. Her breasts spilled free, not too large, not too small. She hissed when his mouth covered one nipple. Evidently, they were sized just right.

"More?" he asked.

She nodded. "Oh, yeah."

"Then ask me nicely." Dark eyes stared at her. "Say, 'Daamin, I want more.'"

"Oh, *really*."

Clever fingers pinched her nipple. Rebekah gasped, the exquisite pain sending a burst of pleasure to her clit. A rapidly swelling clit.

"Daamin, I want more."

"Good."

The Bear's hand slid down her body, delving inside her panties, catching on her curls until his fingers were inside her. Deep inside, no preliminaries. She didn't know how he seemed to understand what she wanted. She wasn't a girl who liked long, dragging minutes of foreplay. When she was horny, she just... wanted. And right away. No preliminaries.

Rebekah moaned as he finger fucked her, opening her legs as wide as the couch and position would allow. Her hands found the buttons of his dress shirt and were soon inside the cloth. Tight muscles flexed under her hands as she ran her fingers all over smooth, heated skin. Down, following the trail of hair on his chest and to the belt of his pants. Her breath caught as he intensified his pace, free hand playing with her breast. When she wrapped her fingers around a hot, pulsing shaft he growled, head thrown back.

She wanted more. "How far are we going to go?"

It was a plea. It was a demand.

4

It wasn't meant to be.

Daamin stiffened, head whipping in the direction of the club and was on his feet in a second. Rebekah hadn't spent ten years with shifters for nothing. She scrambled to her feet, banishing sensual lethargy and swiping her pants off the floor.

"Stay here," he rasped, and was out the door.

She cursed at him, knowing he would hear but probably not care, pulling on her pants and slipping into her shoes before darting after him. Her human ears registered the commotion a few seconds later. Feminine growls and shattering glass. The irritated buzz of a disturbed crowd... bar fight.

Hell, yeah.

She didn't just dive in blindly. She'd been in her share of fights at Tamar's place, had even helped break up a few when she'd bounced nights to help make her way through college. Al had taught her how to defend herself just fine.

Black-clad staff struggled with a male as Asiane hopped up on her counter and streaked across the surface on light feet, a metal bat in her hand. She used her momentum on the last step to leap over the crowd, flying with unusual grace and power even for a Bear.

Rebekah's eyes widened and she sidled along a wall, keeping her back protected. When she was close to the bar, she dove into the crowd, looking for the knot of troublemakers. Security had two, and a third dropped to the ground in the tangle of struggling bodies and crawled away, pushing up to his feet. Rebekah grinned, waiting until the man passed her and stuck out a foot. He went sprawling and Rebekah moved, tackling him and twisting his arms into a hold. He yowled, feet banging the ground.

"Shut up," she said. "It only hurts a little."

"I told you to stay put," Daamin snarled in her ear. "Give me his arm."

She transferred the hold to the Bear. She herself had no legal standing to detain an individual.

"Asiane chased someone out of the club," Rebekah said. "You need to go after her."

Hard eyes glanced at her, then away before a staff member took the human from Daamin and proceeded to drag him to the back. She watched for a second. Only reason to keep the person in the club was if they had contacted police and wanted to get to the bottom of who had started a fight or why. Most times Al just preferred tossing troublemakers out on their ass and making sure they didn't darken his doors for at least two weeks. But then, they were a smallish community. And Rebekah had rarely handled Bears on her own, mostly humans.

"I'll get out of your hair," she said. "Looks like you're gonna have a long night ahead. Nice meeting you."

Rebekah started to walk away when a hand on her arm pulled her to a halt.

"Stay here," Daamin said, dark eyes flaring. "I need to get Asiane. Stay here."

She didn't quite like what she saw in his face- the beginning of male shifter possessiveness, probably unnaturally heightened by the combined stress of sexual frustration and aggression from the fight. If it had been another time, and she was free... she might have pursued something. But she wasn't free to follow her own desires anymore. After tonight, she wasn't free ever again.

So she said what she needed to say to get him out the door to help Asiane. "Sure, go ahead."

It was a testament to his rattled frame of mind- or maybe because he didn't know her- that Daamin nodded and left. Not realizing she hadn't promised diddly squat. Shifters didn't have magical noses for lies like the movies said, but they were a tad more observant than humans when it came to body language and tone of voice. She was always careful not to outright lie, especially since she'd had to play with words a few times in her life- completely non-maliciously, of course- to arrange events to suit her goals.

Rebekah waited a few minutes before strolling out. It was deep night and the chill bit into her skin, her boots crunching on a thin coating of snow on pavement. They'd have a white Solstice, the weather reports said. The city had decorated tall street lamps with holiday banners and strings of winking lights. She'd left her jacket in the car because she enjoyed the rush of icy air, and the pleasure once the heat on her beater vehicle finally activated, warming her bones. Knowing shifter males, Daamin would be pissed to learn she'd ignored his instruction again. But she'd never see him after tonight, so it hardly mattered.

Rebekah slid into her car and started up the engine,

staring sightlessly through the windshield as the heater slowly warmed. Allowed herself to wallow in an unexpected pang of sorrow for a few minutes, and then buried what if's in a deep part of her mind.

***

Daamin ran after Asiane, filling his nostrils with air to catch her scent. Damn her, she wasn't supposed to run after an enemy on her own. Especially since they had suspicions all the recent disturbances in and around the club were skirmishes- a hidden enemy testing their defenses. Maybe testing Asiane. Daamin saw his own grim fears reflected in Asiane's eyes whenever she thought he wasn't watching. They'd been in this country for three years without incident. Three watchful years while they used their smuggled wealth to rebuild a life with new identities. He'd been thorough, even paranoid- no one had ever fled a Daihariin Alpha and lived. They were possessive, cruel. Some more than others, but they always held what they considered theirs and killed anyone who defied them.

Asiane's scent strengthened along with an unfamiliar, acrid tang. Not quite fear, but definitely adrenaline. And not quite human.

He turned a corner and halted right before crashing into his sister. The walking path entered a park, well-lit with tall vintage black poles. Evergreens lined the path Asiane stared at.

"I'm glad you had the sense not to follow him in there," he said, voice sharper than she might have liked.

"I'm not stupid," she said. Asiane turned, eyes hard. For a moment, he looked into his own face before her expression smoothed and she was his little sister again. "This is the third incident this month. Someone is trying me."

"It could be rival shifters seeking territory."

"Could be." That would actually be preferable to the alternative.

"If Daihara had found us, he wouldn't bother with such petty torments. He'd simply strike."

"And if this is Daihara's males, what do you think you're going to do with a bat?"

She smiled, fangs gleaming in the orange fluorescent light. "Oh, I would have used claws, big brother. Come on, let's get back to the club. Shit, I hope no one clumsy fell on all the glass."

They jogged back, senses on full alert. The guard at the door nodded, continuing to direct traffic in and out of the club. Inside, the brief scent of panic had all but evaporated and security was back in place albeit for a few remaining on the floor to supervise cleanup of shattered glass and blood.

"What happened?" Asiane asked her employee.

The guard was human, longish sandy hair an attempt to detract from his ex-military aura. "Blake has a kid in the office. Kid said the one who fled started it."

She blew out a breath. "It wasn't him, he just got in the way. The male attacked me. But the kid might have seen something."

Daamin was already heading to the office, mouth tight. He had nothing but instinct to go by- but it was Daihara's MO. Test defenses before making a strike. See how Asiane and the staff responded to a small annoyance, and plan the real strike based on the gathered data.

He entered the office. The kid- college-aged, or barely older- slumped in a chair, holding an icepack against his face.

Daamin crouched down at his feet. "How's your head?" he asked, injecting sympathy into his voice. "They told me you got clocked a good one."

"Dude came on to me," the kid said, skin flushing. "Fucking-"

Daamin held up a hand. "Yeah, I get it. What did he say to you?"

He jerked a shoulder, his starched white dress shirt crinkling. "Nothing. Just ran into me and I told him to watch where the fuck he was going. Pissed him off and he swung. Who the fuck acts like that? Worse than a girl, man."

Daamin wished he could pinch his nostrils closed- why did humans have to drench their clothing in scents? "Did you see anything else? Was he alone?"

"I didn't see him with a group or anything. Look, I just defended myself and I can't afford to pay any damages. Check the security cams-"

"You're good, man." Daamin rose. "We'll ask you to sign a waiver releasing us of liability, and drinks this week for you and your guys is on the house. Cool?"

"Yeah, that's cool. I ain't no bitch, I don't sue over stupid shit."

Daamin's respect for the kid went up a notch. He looked like a scrawny spoiled waste of college tuition, but his attitude was decent considering he could have been whining about cops and lawyers.

"Take care of him," Daamin said, nodding at the guard and turned to go. Then paused. "The human woman I was with earlier?" He knew the staff would have noticed- it was their job to notice.

"Left," the employee said.

The rush of rage surprised him. That he managed to close the door with barely a click surprised him even more.

Asiane took one look at his face when he joined her behind the bar. "What's wrong?"

"Personal," he replied, curt.

Her eyes narrowed. "Where's the human girl?"

"Gone." His hand flexed, as if he had something crushable in his grip. He looked around, barely registering his desire to smash something. He'd told her to stay put. She'd left him.

"I need to-"

"Let it go, Daamin," Asiane said.

He snarled at her. She returned his snarling with a curl of her lip, allowing a fang to peek out. Her teeth hadn't retracted to human blunt so her own temper was still riding her as well. "You're mating soon- you can't chase pussy anymore."

His rage found a target. He took a step towards his sister. "She isn't pussy. She's-"

"What? She's what?" Asiane's posture changed. If he leaped, she would defend herself. They hadn't had a good knockout, drag-down brawl since she was sixteen and he realized she was too old for him to indulge her that way. Males did not strike females. No matter how annoying.

Daamin exhaled, took a step back. Damnit.

"I liked her," he said, distantly surprised.

Asiane slung an arm around his shoulders. "Yeah, I

liked her too. Piss poor timing. Can't thumb your nose at the Mother's Council now. Would only piss them off and I have a feeling we'll need allies."

He had the same feeling.

5

She hadn't slept well and was compensating with a Venti brewed coffee, double shot, three pumps of caramel, spiked with almond milk. Hot, ridiculously sweet, strong enough to erode paint from a new car and give her a donkey's jolt in the backside simultaneously.

But then, mornings were always like this.

Rebekah stared at her Mac, irritation furrowing her brow. They'd had an appointment, damnit. She'd thought the address C.C. had texted her was the actual studio- but it was only a coffee shop. She'd cased out the block the night before- thus discovering that thrice damned club- and discovered then that he'd pulled a fast one. So was the plan for her to sit tight and wait for him to show up and escort her? Or was he not ready to reveal his super-secret filming location yet? She didn't know, except that sitting here a bare three blocks from Asiane's place- and where she'd walked out on Daamin the night before- irritated her.

Rebekah blew out a breath, finished typing a quick message to C.C. asking him what the hell was going on, in polite words, and sipped on her coffee. Damn if she didn't want to get up and leave.

Her back tingled a second before a deep voice interrupted her thoughts.

"Rebekah?"

Her head jerked up, and she stared at Daamin incredulously. Of all the rotten, ill-timed, glorious luck. The one male she'd never wanted to see again. Not because she didn't yearn to, like ridiculously yearn for such a brief, inconsequential acquaintance, but because she knew she couldn't have him. Couldn't indulge in anything more. Especially not when he intrigued her in a way no other male had for years.

"You were a rebellious daughter."

He took a seat, eyes never leaving hers, placing his hands flat on the table in front of him. As if to assure her that he was harmless. Calm. Yeah, okay. Rebekah knew Bears- especially male Bears. They hated being ignored, even for good cause.

"I didn't give my parents any problems." Not her adoptive ones anyway, and not even her biological after the final straw that sent her into the system. She needed to be blunt. "Look, last night was fun, but I'm not free."

His eyes narrowed. In the bright morning light, he looked clean cut, just another tech yuppie in a V-neck sweater, expensive jacket and tailored jeans. Of course, his clothes fit around a toned body the way most tech yuppies could only dream about, stuck in their cubicles.

"Do you have a male?"

"What's your man got to do with me?" she muttered under her breath.

"What?"

"Never mind." Rebekah grimaced. "My sense of humor

is weird. No, I don't have a man, there are just... circumstances."

"There are no circumstances other than a matebond-which I know you don't have- or marriage that count. You left last night." He leaned forward, then checked the tiny movement.

She smiled at him, deliberately relaxing her body. If she twitched, he would pounce. "Don't let it piss you off. We're just two ships passing in the night. No reason to-"

Long lashes covered his eyes, as if he could hid the subtle glow building. "I want you."

She shut up. Of course, he did, or he wouldn't be street stalking her. Rebekah frowned. "Were you on your way to the club?" She supposed there might be cleanup or admin to do during the day.

He ignored the question. "Spend the day with me. If I can convince you to ignore your circumstances by tonight, then we'll go our separate ways."

Rebekah inhaled. He sounded... serious. "I don't understand what the point would be. For just a night of sex?"

His nostrils flared. "It wouldn't be just." He paused. "I... don't know. I'm not willing to walk away from you yet." Daamin leaned back in his chair, studying her. "Not since fate has you sitting so prettily in my path. What are you doing here?"

"I'm in town for a meeting." She glanced at her email again. "And it looks like I'm being brushed off."

"Cancel then," he said. "Wait one moment."

She watched as he pulled a smartphone out of his blazer pocket, tapped a few keys and put it back. "There, I've canceled mine."

"My Dad is going to kill me. This trip is supposed to be a write-off. What the hell."

She closed the lid of her laptop and switched her cell to silent so she couldn't hear any notifications. The talent wanted to blow Liam Conroy's representative off? Fine. Said rep would spend the day in town playing. Rebekah rose, tilting her head.

"Well, let's party then, mister. But just today. I'm-"

"Not free." He rose, waving a hand. Strong fingers, graceful and oddly familiar. A narrow tapered wrist with a bit of a hair arm peeking out of the jacket sleeve. "Yes, yes. Come."

***

To put him through his *real* paces, Rebekah immediately suggested shopping. "Solstice is right around the corner," she said. "The humans have everything on sale."

He brushed her shoulder, a small touch she was beginning to realize indicated amusement. "You say human as if you aren't one of them."

"Mmmm. You know, I know at least two human women mated to Bears? I guess it changes a girl's perspective of things."

"Intriguing." He led them towards a parking lot. "Are you comfortable traveling in my vehicle? I have a letter of introduction from the Mother's Council from when my Den came here."

She appreciated the offer and the sensitivity behind it. But... she trusted him. Rebekah grimaced. He caught the expression.

"What is it?"

"I trust you, which is stupid as hell." Her glance was warning. "But I used to bounce in a shifter dive bar-country as fuck and my honorary uncle taught me how to handle myself."

He smiled at her. "I don't doubt it. If we are accosted, I'll count on you to guard my back, as I will guard yours."

Rebekah grinned. "Now, that sounds like the perfect first date."

A lesser girl might have blushed, but Rebekah just shrugged her verbal gaffe off. Let him make of it what he willed. But his shoulders relaxed, the remainder of his tension defused. He was now certain she wouldn't try to run.

She got into his car, fully aware it was a classic too stupid to live moment, and realizing she probably didn't care, anyway. She'd been a wild teenager, even after living with Meredith and Dad, so it was way too much to hope she'd be a completely sensible adult. Besides, adulting all the time was way overrated.

"Where to?" he asked. He drove with one hand, draping his right arm over the back of her seat.

She gave him directions to a strip of specialty boutique shops, the kind of places one could find unique handmade items and antiques. She hated mass market gifts, and since Meredith insisted on combining Christmas with Winter Solstice, Rebekah's compromise was to purchase one gift per friend or family member and make the gift personal. Even for the cubs.

They found a parking spot and Rebekah led him into her favorite global goods shop.

He glanced around with every indication of enthusiasm. "I love browsing," he said. "This place reminds me of the bazaars at home."

"Where's home?"

She headed towards a shelf of dolls. Each one had intricately coiffed hair, cultural suits of clothing that appeared handmade when she looked at the seams. Her little sister was old enough for a real doll- one that would teach her how to care for something before Rebekah upgraded her to a puppy or kitten.

"A small country, mostly shifter. It's beautiful, but harsh. And a constant struggle for dominance."

She glanced at him, wondering at the note in his voice. Longing, and a thread of savage anger as if his Bear was riled. Obvious enough emotion even for her human ears.

"Why'd you come here?" Yeah, she was being nosy- but she'd told him quite a bit about herself the previous night, and hell, if he didn't want to answer he didn't have to.

"A dispute over territory. It would have been difficult to keep my sisters sheltered from the repercussions if I lost."

Rebekah watched as he wandered towards a rack of dresses. Long, flowing materials and bright colors. He chose one, lifting it off the rack and examining the cut and pattern. Not bothering to look at a price tag as he folded it over his arm and chose another. Her brow rose. Well, she supposed from the model of his used, but definitely not hooptie car, that he wasn't exactly poor.

"Are you the only male?" she asked, eyeing his selections. He had pretty good taste, in her opinion. He'd skipped over some of the gaudier options.

"Yes, and my mother's eldest cub." Daamin turned and looked at her a moment before lifting one of the dresses. "What do you think?"

"It's not really my style, but the colors are pretty."

His eyes traversed her body. She was in what she called work clothes- slightly more formal jeans, a tank top shell made of blousy fabric instead of plain cotton and a dark, short-waisted blazer instead of leather or denim.

"You would look lovely in anything you chose to wear."

She'd thought he was going to say 'a dress' in the typical male condescending fashion that she hated. As if she would be pretty if she just 'cleaned herself up' a bit. Or, in other words, looked more like a traditional female. The lack of judgment in his tone warmed her even more towards him.

"I'll probably do a dress for Solstice." It would be black or blood red velvet, and corseted. But it would be floor length. Hey, that was dressy enough, even if it wasn't quite the Sunday school version of a dress. She just didn't do flowers, unless they were ink and permanently affixed to her skin.

"I would like to see that," he said, meeting her eyes. He smiled, and she noticed dimples. "With your hair around your shoulders. You would enchant me, I think."

Rebekah licked her lips and stepped away, disguising the movement by choosing another rack of merchandise to peruse. She had to put some space between them. He knew all the right things to say- and damnit. She was a girl, after all. And, evidently, susceptible to all the usual charm type things. It had just taken a male with a brain. Or maybe since it had been a while, her defenses were thin.

"I'd probably put a curse on you," she said after a few moments. Looking over her shoulder, "This is all I want from this place. You want to see a few more shops?"

He nodded, and they checked out, Rebekah taking

tactile pleasure in the quality tissue paper and embossed shopping bags their purchases were placed in. She had a small collection of such bags, and used them on occasion when she needed something a little nicer than a plain plastic grocery sack. The paper was of too good a quality-she hated just tossing it in the trash.

They went through a few more shops. Rebekah relaxed as they chatted, finding him to be a witty, mannerly companion with a dry sense of humor and gentleness of speech. She probed into his past and family, more from insatiable curiosity than anything else. At times, he answered her readily enough, at other times he gently rebuffed her questions through subtle redirection. The little glimpses of steel, plus her memory of his passion the night before, warned Rebekah that no matter how mild mannered he appeared on the outside, he was still a Bear. And, evidently, from an area of the world where territory disputes were fierce, bloody and incessant. She'd be stupid to assume civility meant he was a pushover.

"Would you like lunch?" he asked after they'd been shopping for close to two hours.

"Sure." She wasn't hungry, but his shifter metabolism had to be spurring him right now. Liam packed away whole meals every few hours. "There's a cafe around the corner that does grilled sandwiches and fancy salads."

The walk was brief and once seated, he ordered a steak sandwich and Greek salad. Rebekah had soup and a hot mug of tea, more so that he wouldn't feel the need to feed her while he ate.

"So you have five sisters," she said, dumping a packet of crushed up crackers into her soup. "Asiane seems cool."

She glanced up in time to see the flash of fire in his eyes, a literal glow indicating strong temper. Rebekah froze for a split second, then made herself relax. Never show fear in front of a predator.

"She's okay," he replied, unenthusiastically.

Rebekah blinked. Was this the same male who'd spoken with such fierce protectiveness about his sisters? "I didn't talk to her long last night, but she seems like-"

"I don't want to talk about Asiane." His lip curled, a fang peeking out. "You're with me."

Oh. *Oh.* Rebekah controlled a blink and a grin, suddenly realizing what the issue was. He was jealous. Many shifters were pansexual and gender didn't matter, so he must be wary that she was attracted to Asiane. On the heels of that thought, her stomach sank. Jealousy meant emotions- and this would be their only day together. He wouldn't try and keep her after the day was over, would he? Rebekah frowned in her soup.

"What's wrong?" he asked, voice gentle... but edged.

"My family means everything to me. I owe Dad and Meredith a lot." She met his eyes. "They took me in. Dad's Den, they didn't care I was human. Dad said I was his, so that made me theirs." She glanced away. "I didn't have family until I met them."

"I don't think your father wants you to feel beholden to him. No father who loves his daughter would."

"Doesn't matter. I know what I owe." And she would pay. She would make the price of raising her worth it.

He tilted his head, expression intense. "You love your family. What would you do for them?"

She didn't understand why he asked, but she couldn't look away. Couldn't prevaricate.

What would she do for her family? "I would die for them. I would kill."

He grinned, a fierce flash of white teeth. Not from humor, but from understanding. It hummed between them, a sudden, fierce meeting of minds. For a moment, she felt as if he saw into her, understood her. For a moment, she felt as if she knew him- always had.

And then the moment was gone. But his hand slid across the table and he grasped her wrist. "I think you are a female worth having. Worth keeping."

Oh... oh, shit. She knew what it meant when a Bear male got that look on his face. She'd seen it plenty of times in the Den as couples mated. Rebekah swallowed, pushing down the surge of acceptance, and pulled her wrist away.

"Thanks."

He opened his mouth to speak, eyes narrowing when a cell went off. Daamin paused, excusing himself with a flick of his finger. Rebekah politely turned her attention to her soup, giving him the social version of privacy- where she pretended like she wasn't listening, but was busy thinking very important, engrossing thoughts. Rebekah snorted.

"Talia, why are you-" he stopped speaking, listening to the female on the other side of the conversation.

Rebekah couldn't hear what was said, but she heard the repressed panic in a young adult female voice. She glanced up, watching his face. It went blank, but his eyes burned.

"I'm on my way," he said. "Stay in the office."

Rebekah rose, pulling cash out of her pocket and throwing it on the table. "What's wrong?" she asked. He began to stride out of the cafe, Rebekah on his heels. "Daamin- what's wrong?"

He paused, impatience wild across his face, and then the emotion was gone, controlled. "Rebekah, I'm sorry. My sister is in danger, I have to go to her."

Anger surged. "I'm going with you!"

She didn't know why she cared. Why her own sense of protectiveness rumbled in her chest. Except that she'd been a teenage girl in trouble once and a near stranger had come to her aid.

"It's not you-"

"I was in trouble once, and a stranger helped me." She grabbed his wrist, pulling him out of the cafe. "We're wasting time. I'll ride with you, and if there's trouble, I've got your back."

He yanked her to a halt, whirling her against his chest with restrained violence. Startled, Rebekah had no time to react as lips covered hers in a fierce, drugging kiss. No more than a few seconds; but those seconds branded her.

"A female worth keeping," he said.

And they ran.

6

Daamin drove like a Dragon shifter- that was, without regard to the laws of speed and mortality. Rebekah gritted her teeth and told herself to stop being a pansy, refusing to clutch the door handle. While driving, he activated the Bluetooth and spoke in rapid fire Arabic to Asiane. The conversation was short, their tones crisp.

"We go to pick up the older girls," he said after disconnecting the call. "Asiane and her security will pick up our younger sisters."

"Is your entire family in danger?" she asked.

"I don't know, but we will take too many precautions rather than too few."

In a short time, he'd navigated the city and brought them to a high school, parking and jumping out barely after the car engine was shut down. Rebekah followed. She didn't have shifter speed and strength, but she was toned and fast on her feet and the self-defense training kept her limber.

He crashed through the wide double doors of the

school, students flinging themselves out of his way as he led them to the main office.

Rebekah saw his sisters- the females could be no one else- right away. Slender girls on the cusp of adulthood, dressed in jeggings and long flowing tunics, sheer scarves wrapped aimlessly over their heads. Glossy black hair peeked out, telling Rebekah the scarves were either for decoration or token adherence to cultural tradition. Wide dark eyes glanced over and both girls stood, rushing to Daamin.

"I told them to call the police, but they don't believe us!"

The girls looked pissed, one a little more shaken than the other.

"You'll both come with me," he said.

A school official approached. "Sir, are you their parent?"

Rebekah stifled a snort. Did he look like a freakin' parent? Though she supposed if the school knew they were shifters, it was a reasonable question.

He pinned the woman with a hard stare. "I'm their brother. Have the police been called?"

"No one actually saw-"

"So are you calling my sisters liars?"

Rebekah ran her tongue along her teeth. The woman might want to choose her next words carefully.

"No, of course not. But teenage girls-"

He didn't remain, instead turning and ushering the girls in front of him. One slid away, dashing back to the chairs to grab two backpacks while the other bumped herself up under her brother's arm.

"You'll be fine, Faridah," he soothed. "We go hunting."

Hunting sounded good. She was down for that.

The girl slanted a glance at Rebekah. "Who are you?"

"Backup," she replied. "I'm Rebekah, Clan Conroy."

Faridah stared. "You're human."

"I'm adopted. I know Asiane, too." Not quite true, but she could tell the girl needed reassurances. Rebekah could read between the lines and determine she'd been the victim of some kind of almost assault- she wouldn't want strangers near her right now.

The answer satisfied Faridah and the twin glanced at Rebekah as she approached, saying nothing. But she'd heard.

Rebekah glanced at Daamin as they walked out. He stared at her, expression... odd.

"Conroy?" he asked.

She frowned. "Yeah. It's a good Clan."

"I know. I-" he paused, shook his head. "Never mind. Let's go."

***

"Describe the vehicle," Daamin said as they left the building.

"Blue mini-van, tinted windows," Faridah said, a tremble in her voice. "Some rust around the tires- I don't think it was new. It looked like a mom car, so I didn't think anything when it pulled up."

"I went back to our lockers to get our jackets- it was

making the humans nervous that we didn't have them on," the other said.

Daamin sighed. "Talia- you have to remember things like that. Blending in is one of the best defenses we have."

Rebekah listened closely to the conversation. It was cold enough out that two girls sitting nonchalantly in thin tunics and fluttery scarves would be noticed, like hot house roses blooming merrily in a block of ice. And these days anyone who looked a little 'odd' was immediately labeled a shifter. Bigger cities like Seattle were more tolerant... but this was Tacoma.

"The male who tried to grab me looked like from home, Daamin," Faridah said, voice firming. Maybe because her twin started to retort. Rebekah sympathized. Sometimes you had to drag people back on topic.

"Describe him."

Faridah ran down the description, thorough for a high school girl- even an older high school girl. Rebekah guessed they had to be seniors, but still. How many senior girls could give a professional sounding description of a perp?

"We'll drive around," Daamin said. "Maybe they are still in the area, though I doubt it."

"We only got her away 'cause he was trying to be sneaky," Talia said. "I heard her screaming and ran, roaring. He let her go."

"I don't think he was expecting those moves you showed me," Faridah said.

"Good."

"Were they defensive?" Rebekah asked.

They piled into the car, Rebekah taking a seat in the back so Faridah could sit next to her brother.

"Yes," Talia said. "We aren't warriors. We know enough to stall until help comes."

Rebekah tried to see Daamin's face around the seat. "I know some holds I had to learn to use against shifters- I could show you. Maybe next time you can restrain the guy until help comes so he can't get away with this."

There was silence in the car for a few minutes. Rebekah wasn't dumb- she knew there was something going on here other than some perv trying to lure a teen into a car. These Bears had enemies, and were hiding out, trying to keep a low profile. But whatever their Den may or may not have done, teenage girls weren't to blame.

"I appreciate the offer," Daamin said, words slow as if he were choosing them carefully. "But I do not want to embroil you in our Den's troubles."

She should leave it at that. She'd done the right thing, made the offer. It was none of her business- she had her own Den, her own issues to deal with. She didn't know these people, and had no ties of loyalty of friendship to them.

"I've been in trouble like that a time or two," she said, repeating her earlier words. "I'd like to help- but I don't want to force myself into your Den business. But... I'd like to help. Pay forward the help I've gotten, you know?"

He glanced at her, and Rebekah suppressed a wince and the impulse to tell him to keep his eyes on the road.

"Come to dinner," Talia said. "Let Mama decide."

"Talia-"

"I think that's a good idea, Daamin," Faridah chimed in. "We need allies. We've been too alone for too long."

Daamin sighed. "Just the day, hmm?"

Rebekah grinned. "That was personal, this is just Den

business."

***

They drove the perimeter of the school, circling further and further out before Daamin declared the search over. He headed towards his home. Rebekah took the time to check her phone for any messages from C.C. A notification popped up. She read the terse message, citing a family emergency and that he would contact her to reschedule soon.

Typical. Just typical. "I really hate unprofessional people," Rebekah said, stabbing her finger at the screen. She replied, a message just short of scathing, and slid the phone in her pocket.

"What's wrong?" Daamin asked.

"This guy I'm supposed to meet for my job, I've been trying to corner him for weeks for a meeting so we can get the project- which happens to be on a deadline- rolling and he cancelled again. I'm tempted to call the whole thing off and tell him to go bite himself."

"Ah. Well, hopefully it will resolve itself soon," he said.

"Well, that leaves me free until he contacts me. If he follows form, it won't be for a day or two."

"Then I have you all to myself."

Rebekah remained silent the rest of the trip, realizing she was getting too involved. She could lie to herself and insist her motivations were solely to help the girls with whatever trouble was going on. But it was a lie. She wanted to spend more time with Daamin, enjoyed his solid warmth and shifter sex appeal. Wanted to feel his lips and arms again. Wanted to explore the growing feeling of rightness.

But she couldn't go back on her promise to Gwenafar. Maybe if Daamin... he was a Bear, too, after all... but thinking along those lines was pure fantasy. She shoved the thought away.

The house they pulled up to was in a solid middle class neighborhood, the kind of two-story nondescript frame house with a tall wood fence that any average family might live in. Nothing extravagant to indicate the family was wealthy, and nothing to indicate the inhabitants were Bears. It was so Americana- the perfect disguise.

He pulled into a garage and they all got out. As they walked up to the connecting door, nerves attacked. Rebekah hung back a bit, waiting for Daamin's invitation to enter.

The male turned towards her when she fell back, and took her hand, again lifting it to his lips. "Come in, Rebekah. You're welcome in our home."

It felt like the words meant more than a simple polite social assurance. It felt... she couldn't describe the feeling, other than to say that the last time she'd felt so... settled... was when Meredith and Liam had told her she would be staying with them.

Her heart sank. But she walked in, meeting his eyes for a brief, searing moment.

Female voices rose in a jumble of foreign words, lilting vowels and sharp, guttural consonants. Rapid fire speech from an older female voice. Daamin led her through the kitchen, Rebekah getting only a swift look at a well-appointed, bright room with a recently remodeled magazine look off an open living-dining room combo.

A female in a long dress, wide sleeves with dense embroidery, her dark hair pulled back into a braid, turned.

Sharp black eyes pinned Rebekah, sweeping over her in a thorough look before turning to Daamin.

"Speak English, please, mother," he said.

The female switched languages. "This cannot be tolerated. I didn't want the girls in a public school, and I was right!"

"We'll keep them home." He pulled out his cell, then shut it away at the sound of another vehicle entering the garage. "That is Asiane."

His eldest sister entered the home a moment later with tween girls, bursting through the doors and talking fast.

"English," Daamin yelled over the sudden noise of six females talking.

"Security is posted in the neighborhood and outside," Asiane said. She turned her head to look at Rebekah. "Is there something I should know?"

"Rebekah offered aid on behalf of her Den."

Asiane glanced at him, expression hard. Rebekah said nothing. It was a teeny, tiny, white lie- but, technically, she supposed he could get away with it. She was an official member of a Den, and she *had* offered aid. Traditionally, a Den might back a member up in disputes and then ask questions later behind closed doors. Shifters maintained strength by presenting a unified front.

"What aid?" Asiane asked.

"I'm trained in self-defense," Rebekah said. "I offered to teach the girls some techniques I learned bouncing at a shifter bar."

Asiane held her eyes. "This isn't a coffee date, or a fun little weekend side activity to indulge in and then you go back to wherever you came from."

"I understand. But while I'm here I'll do what I can. It sounds like you need allies."

Asiane's eyes narrowed. "We'll talk about it later. I don't think this is a discussion you and Daamin should have."

The implication being, as the sister looked between Daamin and Rebekah, that neither of them was thinking with their heads. Daamin gave Asiane an ironic look, but nodded.

"We'll sit and discuss over dinner," the older female said. "It is already ready and sitting in the oven- there is no point in waiting since we are all home."

7

Daamin introduced his mother as Muriel before they sat at the table.

"I am happy my son has brought home a female, and an ally. We need both in this house."

"Looks like there are plenty of girls here," Rebekah replied, tongue in cheek.

Muriel raised a brow, eyes glinting. "Yes, but we are all his relatives."

Rebekah ate the food, enjoying the spiced meats and flavorful rice and vegetables. She mostly said nothing, except to answer a few questions Asiane threw her way.

"Should we move?" Faridah asked, picking at her meal.

"No," Daamin said. "This is our home now. We will stay, and we will make it secure. Talia was right- we need allies, or we will be running forever."

They glanced at Rebekah, who looked around the table. "I can't negotiate a Den alliance on behalf of my Clan," she said. "But I can contact my father and... I know a member of the Mother's Council." She'd been reluctant to admit that information- telling them placed a kind of responsibility of her shoulders, because by giving up the information she was de facto volunteering to be a contact.

"Are you able to speak on our behalf?" Daamin asked. Dark eyes watched her steadily, but there was no sense of pressure from him. Only a calm waiting, as if he would accept whatever answer she gave.

"I can talk to her. I can't promise anything. There should be other Dens here in Tacoma. The best thing might be to put you in contact with some of them."

"We were given a list when we applied for permission to settle here," Asiane said. "But it is hard to know who to trust. To... bring anyone into our drama."

Meaning they hadn't wanted to create ties in the community, hadn't wanted to make themselves vulnerable. But now that they knew someone from a Den and the cat was out of the bag... it would be more of a warm introduction, less of a cold.

"I'll make some calls," Rebekah repeated.

Daamin rose. "Thank you. And I'll need a few minutes to take care of some business."

He left the room, touching Rebekah's shoulder as he left.

Asiane watched. "What are you two doing together?"

Rebekah shrugged. "We met up accidently this morning at the cafe near your club. We were just going to spend the day together since we were both at loose ends as far as work."

"What are your long-term plans?" Asiane set down her fork.

"My son looks at you with respect," Muriel said.

Discomfort instantly curdled the food in her stomach. "I think he's just cool that I offered to help."

"Mmm. Is your Den an old one?"

Rebekah went through several responses, discarded many, and ended up with, "We've been around."

"Well. Allies are good, especially allies with deep roots. History is important, almost as important as intentions."

"I... agree."

Asiane snorted. "Stop mate-hunting, mother."

"Strength lies in numbers, and in the power of your extended kin. You should both be mate-hunting."

Asiane slanted a look at Rebekah. "You said you had some moves to show the girls? Come, we could all use a few minutes of fresh air. The backyard is secure."

***

Family came first, but part of his duty in caring for his family was maintaining the health of his business. So he took a few moments to respond to email, reschedule the appointment he'd cancelled. The tone of the representative was increasingly testy these days- and deservedly so. With a project deadline coming soon, Daamin knew he was the one holding up progress.

And then... the human woman in his home was Rebekah of Clan Conroy. Shifters sometimes used their Clan names in lieu of a family surname when introducing themselves. It wouldn't be unusual for Rebekah to have picked up on that habit.

But how many R. Conroy's were there? Besides the R. Conroy staying in his living room, who spent the last several hours suppressing colorful language when describing the individual who kept cancelling meetings on her... as he'd been cancelling meetings with R. Conroy.

Daamin didn't quite know what to do with the newfound knowledge, so he decided to carry on as if he hadn't learned anything, and allow events to unfold.

Besides, there was also the other email, the one he'd been pretending wasn't sitting in the top of his folder, bolded, waiting for his attention. With an unexpectedly heavy heart, he opened it, forcing himself to read through the brief lines.

"*We've reviewed your request and are happy to match you with a female from a suitable Den, meeting the requirements you specified. We feel the genetic diversity you bring to our Territory is especially beneficial, and look forward to similar requests from your Den mates as they come of age. We've attached the file of the female who has agreed to the match. We assure you she is of good family, well-educated, healthy and capable of bearing cubs and is also hardy of character and capable of defending self and kin. Please notify us ASAP so arrangements may proceed forthwith.*"

Gritting his teeth, he sent a brief reply. "*Please commence arrangements for after the Solstice holiday. I am pleased with your choice and look forward to making her acquaintance.*"

He didn't even open her file. He didn't care. No matter what she looked like, or how poor her temperament, he needed allies. And protector mates for his sisters. He would sacrifice himself to get a solid foothold in a local Clan to find them ideal males.

As he shut down the laptop, thinking of the vibrant human female waiting for him in the living room, he realized the taste in his mouth was ashes.

***

Rebekah demonstrated a series of holds, showing the girls how to restrain a man no matter what size, take him down to the floor or slam him against a wall and use his attempts to escape against him, causing pain. They weren't difficult, they were all about using leverage and learning the exact amounts of pressure to apply to cause anything from discomfort to excruciating pain. The grass was damp and slippery from the sprinkling of snow the prior evening, so she had to pay close attention to her balance. Even if she was the teacher and they the pupil- they were Bear. And she was human.

The screen door squeaked open and banged shut just as Talia brought Rebekah down to the grass, twisting her arms in a way that made Rebekah wonder if she'd done something to offend the girl.

"That looks... uncomfortable," Daamin's voice said from above her.

"Talia appears to be retaining my instruction quite well," Rebekah said into the grass.

A snort and giggle later, and the twin released Rebekah, who pushed to her feet, subtly moving her shoulders and suppressing her wince. Everything felt intact, but one never knew with Bears.

She turned, meeting Daamin's eyes. He watched her, hands in his pockets, expression inscrutable. "I think I heard your cell go off," he said. "Maybe it's your client?"

Rebekah headed inside, a hound scenting blood. She'd left the cell at her place on the table. Dishes were already cleared, disappointing her a bit. She'd kinda wanted to finish the meal. Muriel poked her head out of the kitchen.

"Rebekah, I put your dinner in a container. A girl with your shape needs plenty of calories."

"She thinks you're too skinny," Asiane said, entering

the house.

Rebekah snorted, typing a message on her cell. "Skinny shaming now, are we?"

Muriel sniffed. "My food- it will make a proper female of you."

She didn't doubt it. "Ha! Done avoiding me, huh? I guess my last message must have worked. Sometimes you just can't be nice."

"No, indeed," Daamin said, voice silky smooth as he joined his sister. "The girls will continue to practice for a few more minutes. Rebekah, don't allow us to hold you past your time. I know you have commitments."

The brushoff might have bothered her, but she didn't think he meant it like that, they were far too eager for her help in contacting potential allies, and he was absolutely right- she needed to get back to her hotel and get some work done.

"Yeah. Business waits on no woman."

"I'll take you to your hotel."

She met eyes the rich color of the carob powder Aunt Norelle had tried to fob off on her once. Eyes she could sink into, especially when they looked at her as if...

"Thanks," she said, cutting off the thought. "I'll grab my dinner." Rebekah grinned. "Can't let food go to waste."

***

The ride to the hotel was mostly quiet. She ignored an occasional sidelong glance, the line of her body acutely aware of his presence a few inches away. Well- not that a body could be aware of anything. But sometimes it felt as if her body had a mind of its own.

Desires of its own, despite her better judgment.

Desires that had her asking him up for a drink before sending him on his way. And trying to sound all casual like it was just some coffee between new friends, an after dinner bit of socializing.

He regarded her for a moment, gaze steady. "Alright, Rebekah. I'll come up for a... drink."

It wasn't like this was the first time she'd sweet-talked a man into no strings attached sex- and it wasn't like Daamin was unwilling. She just had to brush against his arm to feel the tension in the hard bicep. The third time she 'brushed' against him in the elevator, he grabbed her upper arm, pulling her against his chest and staring down at her with the calm, knowing eyes of a male who'd been onto the game all along- and probably thought he was the one in charge, anyway.

"Rebekah, did you really want coffee when we get to your room?"

She frowned up at him. He wasn't that much taller than her, but the self-contained assurance in his movements made him seem taller. More... dominant. But not in an asshole way.

"Of course I want coffee. There are certain social niceties-"

"You don't look like a female who cares about social niceties."

She considered him. Well, when she'd been a teenager he would have been right. A sullen, rebellious to any kind of authority teenager. But she had mostly grown out of that, assured enough of her own personal power and autonomy that she didn't need to be rebellious any more.

At least not for the sake of rebellion.

"There's more to me than my looks."

He smiled, the dimples slowly deepening. "The looks are very pleasing, though."

She sighed, pleased, but rolled her eyes. Males were so superficial, but they almost couldn't help themselves. Still, it was nice to feel appreciated.

Rebekah led him through the blue carpeted hallway, running fingers along the textured wallpaper because she enjoyed the tactile contact. Slid the keycard into the small bedroom and walked in, Daamin at her heels.

"Make yourself comfortable," she said, dropping her purse on the counter and moving to the fridge. She always booked hotels with kitchens because she was a late night snacker and preferred her snacks be actual food rather than chips. Liam had spoiled her, she supposed.

"I have white wine."

She turned and he was right there, plucking the small bottles from her hands. "I don't need wine to want you," he said.

"You can't say things like that to me," she said, unresisting when he took her hand and pulled her towards the sleek grey couch.

"Why not?"

"Because it makes me-" want things. Believe things that weren't possible.

He pulled her down onto his lap, a finger rubbing her bottom lip. "Makes you vulnerable? I am the one who has been lured." He lowered his head, pressing a kiss against her neck as he swept her hair to one side. "Seduced."

Rebekah shivered, body clenching as his teeth nibble at

her skin. "Who is seducing whom?"

He slid the jacket from her shoulders, baring her arms in the business tank top. Rebekah shifted on his lap, straddling him, and strong hands gripped her waist, running up and down her rib cage as loamy eyes lightened to an umber burn. Between her thighs, even covered by the layer of denim, she felt his hardness. Not that she needed to feel it. The pressure of his hands, the brightness of his eyes and the way his mouth latched onto her neck a second time, nips intensifying into tiny bites...

Rebekah buried hands in his hair. "Don't bite me," she warned. "Not with Bear teeth."

"Fangs," he said against her neck. "Kiss me then. Distract me from thinking thoughts I shouldn't be thinking."

She distracted him real quick, worried about those thoughts. But then worry evaporated because all she could think of was how she wanted more of his hands, now underneath her tank and cupping her breasts. Wanted them all over her naked body. Her hips ground against him.

"I don't need foreplay," she said, voice harsh. "I just want you inside me."

Daamin rose, Rebekah's legs wrapping around his waist as he walked them to the bed. He paused long enough to kick off shoes and then peeled the clothing from her body, the slow steadiness of his personality gone. In front of her stood a male intent on devouring. When she was bare, legs splayed open before him, he did pause, running a finger along her slit, dipping it into her channel. Rebekah hissed, hips arching.

"No teasing," she said.

He unbuttoned his shirt, discarding pants and then was

before her, deep golden brown skin silk taut over lean muscles, dark hair a delicious spatter across chest and arms, the line of it trailing down to a thick nest at his groin. Rebekah licked her lips, sat up and wrapped her hand around his length. He inhaled sharply, head lolling back as his eyes closed. Hot, thick in her hand, pulsing with life and energy. His eyes opened.

"Now who is teasing?"

Not her. Rebekah flipped over onto her knees, knowing what she wanted. Him buried deep inside, the angle so sharp pain blended in pleasure.

Looking over her shoulder at a male gone still with desire, she said, "Take me. No teasing allowed."

Hands locked around her hips. Rebekah spread her legs even wider, arching the small of her back as his cock nudged her entrance.

"Hard," she said. "Fast. No mercy."

A hand buried in her hair. "I'm a Bear. I could hurt you."

"I enjoy the pain."

A sudden sting on her buttocks, a sharp ache as he pushed inside her, no preliminaries, just a male following instructions.

Rebekah gasped, breath gone for a moment. A broken, throaty laugh escaped her lips as he withdrew, then pounded inside her again, the stroke accompanied by another stinging slap.

"Oh, fuck. Yes, again."

She moaned, the force of his body slamming into hers exquisite. He played with her, long sweet strokes followed by staccato, nearly harsh strokes, the head of his cock angled perfectly against her inner spot. He controlled her hips effortlessly, squeezing as she tried to shift, bringing her right back to him.

Then he leaned over her, hands sliding around her front to accost her breasts, plucking at the nipples and twisting. Not gentle.

"That's for disobeying me twice," he said. He ground inside her, rhythm punishing. Mocking her endurance as her arms began to tremble from the fatigue of drawn-out pleasure.

Rebekah gritted her teeth, refusing to give him the satisfaction of hearing her cry out. "Not yours," she said.

"Really?" His voice mocked her. Teeth in her neck, not quite breaking skin. Cock in her body, fingers squeezing her breasts. "It feels like you're mine. It feels like you're trying not to scream my name."

She couldn't respond, couldn't contradict the ragged vow in his voice. Her orgasm crested, pussy clenching tight in waves of sensation.

"Good," Daamin said, voice dark. Satisfied. "Now it's my turn."

He fucked her for several more strokes, Rebekah whimpering when it almost reached the point where her knees wanted to collapse. She couldn't remember when she'd been used so well, given so much pleasure and with so little effort.

A hoarse cry over her and hot seed filled her body. He emptied himself in her body, breathing harsh. Slid out with a groan, juices crawling down her thighs. A kiss on her buttocks, the soft caress of his hand as if to thank her.

Rebekah crawled forward until she could drape herself over a fat pillow and collapsed. "A nerd in the streets and a beast in the sheets," she muttered in the pillow.

Weight settled next to her, the feel of his gaze on the back of her neck. "Are you a cuddler?"

Bears. Rebekah sighed, lifting her head and he smiled at her, fangs still a little too sharp for her liking, but happy. Him, not the fangs. Daamin positioned their bodies until they were spooning, the shifter post coital need for touch evident in how he draped both an arm and leg over her.

"Shifters," she said.

He nipped her jaw. "I resent the nerd comment."

8

She fell asleep on him. Pride swelled in Daamin's chest. Only a well satisfied female, and one who felt safe in his protection, would fall asleep so easily. After a while he left her in the bed, decision made, and sent a quick email to the Mother's Council.

He didn't need their arranged bride. He had the perfect one waiting for him in the bed.

***

The harpsichord woke her before the sun drug itself out of bed. A light under the bathroom door and the sound of a shower told her where Daamin was. The stickiness between her sore thighs told her she'd soon be joining him. After she took care of the messages on her phone.

Rebekah tapped on the notification, a text from Gwenafar. Read the terse two sentence instruction and her pleasant mood dissolved.

:*Your intended mate reneged. You need to come home so we can salvage the situation. He was perfect for you.- Gwenafar*:

Rebekah replied, a grim stone of acceptance settling low in her belly. :*Does it matter? Find another one.*:

She didn't have to wait long for a reply. :*No. Come home today, we'll strategize. I mean it. This one was a perfect match. I won't be so easily brushed aside. It's an insult.- Gwenafar*:

And that was the real issue. The male had accepted, and then summarily rejected Gwenafar's relation. Though Rebekah was certain Grams thought the match was perfect, if she said so. Grams wasn't a liar. Glancing at the bathroom door as the water shut off, Rebekah knew she'd either have to scramble to sneak out, which she didn't have enough time to do, or get Daamin to leave long enough for her to pack up and vamoose.

She bent over the counter, hand pressed into her stomach as a ripping pain tore through her. She wasn't sure if it was physical, or the anguish of leaving. Anguish she had no business feeling. Just because he seemed perfect didn't mean he was. After all, two days of acquaintance wasn't nearly enough rope to hand a man in order to hang himself. Most of them could maintain good behavior for at least three days.

"Are you ill?" Daamin asked, voice sharp when the door opened suddenly.

Rebekah straightened. "Just some cramps." She tried to smile. "Probably premenstrual."

He froze in the act of drying his hair. Another towel was slung loosely around his hips, a cute sign of modesty. Daamin cleared his throat. "Are you on birth control?"

"Yes." She'd dug out her old, unopened pack of pills from last year's prescription just last week when she'd decided it was time to get some groove back.

He let out a breath. "Good. You would make a good mother, Rebekah. But... I cannot have cubs outside of a mating."

She nodded, not offended by the quiet words. She didn't know why he thought she would make a good mother, but she was definitely off the mating market.

"You hungry?" she asked. "There's a diner down the street that does Belgian waffles."

He approached, lowering his head to place a sweet morning kiss on her lips. "That is a female's way of telling a male to go hunt her breakfast."

Rebekah smiled, though with every word and light touch her mood darkened. "Yeah. With strawberries."

"Coming right up, *habibti.*"

He pulled on his clothing and left the room a few minutes later, Rebekah puttering around as if she was about to take a shower. She let herself take a five-minute shower because she didn't want to go home with the scent of another male on her skin, and because she needed to make herself wait long enough to ensure he'd cleared the immediate area.

After a quick dry and throwing on jeans and a cable sweater, she threw her things in her bag and left the room, penning a quick note for him at the front desk. She didn't want him to feel disrespected, just understand she was trying to make the break clean and that she would honor her word and try her best to send allies his way.

But it would be impossible to see him again.

Thirty minutes on the highway and she realized the pain in her stomach was sorrow.

***

He read her note. Refused to allow himself to think as he drove home, Rebekah's breakfast in his hand. He placed it on the table- one of the girls would eat it, and went to his room for clean clothing. When he emerged, Asiane was sitting next to the tray of food, sniffing at it.

"You never eat..." Her voice trailed off as she looked at him. Hard. Then swore. "Goddamn, you slept with her."

He sat down, staring at the strawberries. They look like tiny little organs floating in congealed blood. "Yes."

Asiane's eyes widened. "You always said you wouldn't give your virginity to a female unless you were mated."

For a split second he wanted to pounce on his sister. Then he reined himself in. She wasn't rubbing his vow in his face. He'd enjoyed sexual play with plenty of females since he was an adult, but he had always stopped, not wanting to give that one last thing to some random female. He had little to offer. Despite the success of the business he and Asiane ran, mating him would come with a world of responsibility and even danger. There was little to make up for it, but he could at least promise his mate and wife that he would be faithful. That there were no others to compare her to. That he belonged to her, and her alone.

"Where is she?" Asiane's voice softened.

"She left."

His sister rose to her feet, walking an agitated circle around the table. "But... why? She didn't strike me as shallow. She said-"

"I know what she said." He withdrew the note from his pocket, placed it on the table.

Asiane snatched it up. " *Daamin, please don't hate me. I*

told you when we met I was not free. The truth is, a mating has been arranged for me and I can't go back on my word. I owe everything to the Den that raised me. I promised you aid, and I will fulfill that promise to the best of my ability. My uncle owes me a favor- I'll send him to you. I think it's best if he is your contact. All the best, Rebekah.' "

Daamin looked up at his sister's sigh. She didn't sound surprised. "She told me that first evening. I'd just assumed she wouldn't be any different to you than any of the other females you dallied with."

He said nothing. What could he say? The female he'd felt such a strong connection to had walked out on him, had placed duty to her Den over him. Daamin was almost certain she shared the strength of his feelings. It was hard to gauge with humans, but when she looked at him...

Asiane studied him. "You seem... calm."

He rose. "I know where she is. And who she is. She won't escape so easily."

***

Rebekah sighed, half listening to Gwenafar's civilized rant. She'd walked in the door of her apartment only to find her Grandmother sitting at the table, tea, tablet and muffins in front of her.

"Didn't know you had a key, Grams," Rebekah said.

The female snorted without looking up. "Of course, I have a key."

"So tell me what's going on."

And then the rant had begun. Rebekah picked at a blueberry-raspberry muffin. "Ok, what do you want me to do? If the guy changed his mind-"

"He needs to meet you. Once you two meet, I'm certain you'll hit it off."

"Why are you certain?"

"Liam would like him."

Rebekah's eyes narrowed. The answer was evasive. Grandmother was up to something. "How do you know? Just who is this guy, anyway?"

Gwenafar waved a hand. "I have a file, but I thought a blind first date would be more fun."

"Okaaaay." Not her idea of fun, but fine. Elders needed their little amusements, after all. "I think it's time for another tattoo."

Gwenafar stared at her, distaste flitting across her face. "What? What are you talking about?"

Rebekah shook her head. "Never mind." She stood up. "Whatever you want, Grams. I need to do some work and then I'm taking an early nap." The drive had drained her and she was feeling more than a little sleepy.

The older female sniffed as Rebekah passed her. "Who is that scent?"

She hurried into her bedroom and shut the door.

Settling on her bed, she opened her laptop and replied to the email waiting for her. C.C. requesting an earlier meeting than they'd agreed. But this time, she was the one to cancel. No way was she going back to Tacoma right now. Dad would have to handle it. She let him know Liam Conroy would be in touch soon, and sent an email to her Dad updating him on the situation- both work related and personal, and asking for a day off. Then she curled under the covers and went to sleep.

It was the only escape from the gnawing pain she tried to pretend didn't exist.

***

Three fat, pure white candles of varying heights decorated the mantle. Rebekah placed evergreen boughs around them and added little glittery things made of gold. Meredith put finishing touches on the tree. They'd finished decorations at the Conroy house and were now at Alphonso and Tamar's log 'cabin' in the woods. Alphonso wasn't big on the decorations and left it to the females, and Tamar preferred to cook rather than play with lights and bright colored balls.

Rebekah left the living room and went into the kitchen, drawn by the smell of lasagna. The blend of spicy sauce, three different meats and five cheeses should have made her stomach rumble. But as good as it smelled, she just wasn't hungry.

Tamar turned her head, pointing to the kitchen table. "Sit. We need to talk."

Rebekah obeyed, leaning an elbow on the warm wood. "What did I do?"

"You tell me."

Tamar slipped her hands into two fluffy oven mitts and opened the door, taking the first, then the second, glass pan out of the oven. She adjusted the temperature and timer and in went two sheet pans of rolls. After discarding the mitts and taking a large wooden salad bowl out of the fridge, she sat down, facing Rebekah.

"Talk," the woman said, staring Rebekah down.

She folded her arms. "About what?"

"Al says you smell like young."

It took Rebekah a second, then she shook her head. "Hell no, I don't. I'm on the pill."

Tamar smiled, leaning back, expression satisfied. "You didn't deny you met someone."

Rebekah rolled her eyes. "I meet several someones throughout the course of a year."

"Not this year, you haven't. I've been watching. You're around mating age and if you think Gwen isn't chomping at the bit to get you mated off to some-"

Rebekah coughed. "Well."

Tamar's chocolate eyes widened. "I knew it! Have you met him?"

"No. They're still in talks. He backed out a few weeks ago, but she talked him back into it. He can't clear his schedule yet, though." Which would have rankled, except these days she didn't seem to care about anything but work, and even her interest in that had paled. Rebekah shrugged. "I don't care. I'm doing it for-"

"If you say for the Clan, I'll beat your ass, girl. You don't have to mate for the Clan."

"What are you talking about?" Meredith asked, entering the kitchen.

"See what you did," Rebekah said.

Liam had agreed, despite his anger at his mother, to not say anything to Meredith, because that's how Rebekah wanted it. But the cat would be out of the bag sooner or later.

"Your mother-in-law is trying to mate this girl off and have some new cubs, that's what."

"What?" Outraged green eyes tore into Rebekah. "You

didn't tell me? How long has this been going on?"

They argued back and forth for the next several minutes, talking Meredith out of calling Gwenafar and Challenging her to the Circle. She did call her mate, and tore a strip off him. A text pinged her phone as Meredith was yelling.

It was Dad. :*Thanks a lot- Dad*:

Rebekah grinned. She could just imagine the sourness of his tone. :*Hey, can't you control your mate?*:

He, of course, had no reply to that.

"That's not even the worst thing, Mere," Tamar said, arms folded. Then the oven beeped and she surged out of the chair to grab bread rolls.

Meredith rounded on her best friend. "What else is there?"

"Al says she smells pregnant."

Meredith stared at Rebekah, then disconnected her call. "Bathroom. Now."

Rebekah rolled her eyes, unmoving. "What, you think Tamar has a handy stack of tests in her bathroom?"

"Yup," Tamar said, breaking open a roll and slathering it with butter. "A whole box. Less than a quarter each on the internet. Handy to have around. Do it quick, the kids will be back soon and they are nosy as all get out. And if Al gets confirmation, you know he's gonna tell Liam. That male don't know how to keep his mouth shut."

"Fuck." Rebekah allowed her foster mother to drag her to the bathroom. "Look, I'm on the pill. There's no way-"

"Since when have you been on the pill?" Meredith opened the bathroom door, shoved Rebekah inside and followed after her. She crouched down to the cabinet under the sink. "There should be a box and a sleeve of pee cups... here. It's a strip. Just pee in the cup and dip it for five seconds."

Humoring Meredith, Rebekah went through the motions, watching in fascination as the tiny little strip of paper turned pink.

"See?" Rebekah said. "Two lines. That's negative."

Meredith stared at her, deep green eyes both calculating and mirthful. "Two lines is positive."

"What? That's not what the..." she picked up the foil package. "...oh, shit." Rebekah sat down on the toilet seat, hard. "What the fuck? How the hell did this happen? I'm on the pill."

"You haven't mentioned an OB/GYN appointment in over a year."

"I didn't need one. I had a leftover pack. I've been taking one every day."

"Rebekah, did you check the expiration date?"

"What? They *expire*? Since when do pills *expire*?"

Meredith sighed. "I work with teenagers for a living, and I hold hands every year while girls and boys go through pregnancy scares. There isn't anything I don't know about the failure rates of birth control now. Oh, Brick. You are never boring. We're going to have to tell the male your grandmother has arranged for you. He might not want to go ahead-" she paused. "The father? Is he a Bear?" A lilt at the end of the sentence told Rebekah what Meredith hoped for.

"Yup."

"Oh, dear god, thank you." Meredith sat down on the edge of the tub. "That's the only thing that will keep Gwenafar from throwing a complete fit. A cub. That's the whole point, after all. Cubs."

"I'm pregnant." Rebekah stared at the strip.

Meredith leaned forward and took her hand, squeezing it. "It's okay, baby. You're responsible and you have plenty of family. This will be fun, don't worry."

9

"She's agreed to a Solstice mating ceremony," Gwenafar Conroy said. If any more satisfaction permeated her voice, it would ooze through the cell.

"Fine. Email me the details."

"Absolutely. Have a good day."

Daamin disconnected, leaning back in his chair. His office was cramped, dark and windowless, a converted storage room in the converted warehouse he'd turned into an internet studio. There were several stalls including his own that he leased to different online entrepreneurs who'd decorated their sets and filmed for YouTube and other ventures.

His office probably wasn't anything like Liam Conroy's. Nor like Cassius', the millionaire tech genius and mate of his soon to be sister-in-law. He preferred it that way. The family businesses brought in enough income to support them all comfortably, but not enough wealth to attract undue attention. He would have to deal with his Clan at some point- signs that the Daihariin were in town were ever increasing. He knew it was only a matter of time before another attempt was made to snatch one of his sisters and take them back home. The Alpha would never forgive Daamin for stealing three of the Clan's most desirable females away from them, not to mention the younger girls who would be adults in a handful of years.

Shuffling through his email, he pulled up the file sent him by the Mother's Council weeks ago, accessing the picture of the mate they'd chosen for him.

Rebekah Conroy. R. Conroy. It was a professional shot, likely a part of her press kit for Liam's production studio. Hair a loose tail over one shoulder, subtle makeup and a black leather jacket that tried to look like a blazer. A hint of irony in her eyes and the tiny curve of her lips. It screamed rebel to a smart male.

The last few weeks had been a strain. He knew where she was, he wanted to contact her- but then again he didn't, he wanted to let this charade play out until the end, see what she would choose. Go along with an arranged mating in order to fulfil duty? Or back out and choose him first? Either choice, he was conflicted. On one hand, a female who understood family loyalty and would fight for the good of the Den- that was what he wanted. Needed. But Daamin the male wanted a mate who put him above all others.

Daamin sighed. It was selfish of him, and likely childish as well. Life didn't always fit easily into pretty little boxes, and whatever choice she made, there would be benefits and repercussions. Except, in this case, she wasn't aware that duty and heart could merge.

He wasn't going to tell her. Not yet. Even though Asiane disapproved of the deception. Even though his Bear urged him to go to his female and claim her, and stop playing these mental games with himself.

A knock on his office door and his personal assistant popped his head in. "Daamin, did you want to shoot the episode today? And we still have to review the script Conroy sent us."

He rose. "Is he still asking that I reveal my identity on the special?"

Logan's eyes widened. "Of course. And you have to admit, it would be the perfect venue. The amount of traffic driven to the site from being featured... plus once all the ladies see your handsome mug-"

Daamin grimaced. "I'm soon to be mated. And to his daughter."

Logan stared. "Man, if I didn't know you, I'd think you were either joking or gone off the deep end."

They left the office together. "Tell him yes."

"Hell, yeah. You sure? You've been all secret squirrel for two years now."

Yes, but now he had the backing of an influential Den in a powerful Clan- and the skirmish attacks on the bar made it clear that someone in his enemy's employ had either guessed or confirmed Jaafir whereabouts already. With the mating would come resources to help him eliminate the danger from old enemies once and for all. If Rebekah didn't refuse to go through with the ceremony when she saw him.

"I'm sure. It's a mutual mating present." His future mate just didn't know it yet.

***

"What do you want to do?" Liam asked her.

They knelt in the backyard winter garden, carefully tending shoots of greens designed to withstand the seasonal cold. A greenhouse covered the plants, protecting them from snowfall that was due any day now.

"I guess I'll make a doctor appointment," she said, staring sightlessly at the ground.

He touched her cheek. Rebekah looked up when the pressure increased. "You don't seem happy about being pregnant," Dad said. "Do you want the cub? You can always have an abortion."

Rebekah growled. Fierce denial, the beginning of protective rage rose in her throat. "I would never do that!"

Calm eyes studied her. "I know you won't. I needed to get a response out of you. You've been listless these last few weeks."

She scowled. "I've done my job."

"Yes. But you don't seem to take any pleasure out of it anymore. You don't have to go through with the mating. He might not even want to- now."

Rebekah rose, brushing off the knees of her pants. "I don't really care one way or the other. I'm going to go make tea."

The water had just come to a boil when Dad entered the kitchen. "That's the problem, you know. It's not normal. You're one of the most anti-apathetic people I know. Rebekah," his voice gentled. "Have you spoken to the father?"

She filled a strainer with two heaping tablespoons of loose leaf tea, wondering why her vision was blurry. She blinked several times. "No."

"I think you should, Brick."

She turned, reluctantly. He only used her nickname

when he really, really wanted her attention.

"You know what you look like to me? Like a female who was beginning to bond, and it was cut off too soon. Plus add the hormones from pregnancy... I think you should talk to the father. Is he a good guy?"

The last question was asked all too casually, her Dad leaning against the counter and crossing his arms as if he was trying to portray nonchalance. She eyed him. He was doing pretty good, but he wouldn't quite meet her eyes- which meant he was holding back the alpha nature to defend and protect. And rend the offending male in question to pieces.

"He takes care of his family. He- I'm pretty sure he has a job of some kind."

"Well, call him and see what he says about all this. He deserves to know he has a cub. And maybe there's a happier resolution to all this than mating you off to a stranger- even if he is willing to accept another male's cub."

Rebekah thought about it that evening. And thought hard. Daamin hadn't once talked about mating and long-term commitments, had even said he didn't want cubs with a female outside of a formal mating, but he'd seemed to like her well enough. And they'd been talking Den ties and all that shifter political stuff. Uncle Boden had agreed to meet with him after the holidays and talk business. The local Den could use new members, or even satellite members to expand their territory. All the Council wanted was for her to mate a Bear and have a cub to strengthen and diversify the genetic lines. Well, she was on her way to doing one-half of that. Why couldn't she make a permanent commitment with Daamin? If a stranger, why not him? Why had she been assuming the only way to go was to let Grams pick a mate for her?

All she had to do was convince him she was mate material.

Rebekah dialed Liam. "Dad? I'm going to Tacoma. I'll take over any errands you need for the episode while I'm there." She'd need plenty of work to keep her distracted while she waited on Daamin to make a decision.

***

Daamin stared at the text, wondering if a joke was being played on him.

:Will be in town soon. Let's finally meet up and go over script. I'll have a few free hours.- R. Conroy:

But there was no way, unless Gwenafar had told her- and the Elder had insisted she was keeping her mouth shut until the mating ceremony, for reasons of her own- that Rebekah knew the Chemical Confectionist and Daamin Jaafir were the same person. He grimaced as the thought slid through his head. He hated the nickname, but it had stuck, especially in social media and once his skeleton staff got ahold of it- they'd gleefully branded him without caring a single whit if he liked it or not. That's what he got for being a laid-back employer. People thinking they had actual creative freedom.

He texted her back, giving a time and date and sat back to think about what he was going to do now that the Bear was out of the bag.

***

Rebekah sat in front of Daamin's house in a

nondescript midsized rental car. It was the only thing she could think of- the club wasn't open this time of day and she had no idea how to track him down otherwise. But he had to come home sooner or later. Several times she had to slow her breathing, force herself to remain calm. What would he say? Would he be angry? Would he think she'd gotten pregnant on purpose, or lied about her birth control? She'd done her own reading about the efficacy of expired pills over the last several days, as well as the effectiveness of human hormonal birth control when Bear genetics were involved. The latter was inconclusive, but the former... evidently the hormones in pills that were old started to break down after time and stopped working. She hadn't known that.

Demonstrably.

Rebekah closed the lid of her laptop, unable to focus on work and discarded the idea to just walk up to the house and knock on the door. If Daamin didn't want to see her, it would be less awkward if his family didn't know she was in town. Closing her eyes for just a moment, she fell asleep.

***

The sound of the car door opening jerked Rebekah into wakefulness. Asiane stood there, staring down at her with an inscrutable expression.

"Funny seeing you in this part of town," the sister said.

Rebekah shook her head, trying to fully wake up, and rummaged in the passenger seat for a tin of mints. Stalling.

"I wanted to see Daamin."

"We've been watching you nap for the last hour.

Mother couldn't take it anymore. Come in and eat, he won't be home for a while."

There was no way to refuse without insulting her potential future sister-in-law, and she was hungry. Twisting to reach into the back seat, she grabbed clean, empty Tupperware containers.

"I brought back the containers," she said.

Asiane's brow rose. "Miracles. Some people have no manners these days- glad to know chivalry isn't dead."

The female Bear leaned down, long dark hair falling over her shoulder in thick waves, and grabbed Rebekah's wrist. "Come on."

The block was relatively quiet- but as soon as she stepped inside, contained chaos reigned. The younger girls ran through the house making loud, screeching noises. One in a Princess dress, the other dressed like a movie assassin. Muriel yelled, voice coming from the kitchen while one of the twins yelled back. A blend of Arabic and English.

"Mama caught Faridah switching the spice containers," Asiane said. "Don't mind the yelling. It's normal."

Evidently Asiane had been instructed to come fetch her, because Muriel only gave Rebekah a brief glance before waving toward a seat at the table. Rebekah inhaled, the roasting meat and rich spices causing her mouth to water.

"Oh, man, I think I just got my appetite back," she said in a half moan.

Muriel glanced over her shoulder, a longer look. "Are you skinnier than you were last time? That's no good."

"I've lost a few pounds." Rebekah grimaced.

Muriel sniffed. "You will have dessert, too. I never let

my girls leave the table without dessert. A female needs to maintain her strength. Even human females."

Some unspoken cue and all the girls rushed to the table. Muriel sat next to her, explaining different dishes and spooning bits of food onto Rebekah's plate. There was a lull in the conversation as everyone began eating. Muriel leaned closer and said,

"So. When are you telling Daamin you are pregnant?"

10

Muriel took delight in banging on her back and Asiane shoved a glass of water under her nose so she could wash down the rice she was choking on. A long, heated discussion ensued and before Rebekah knew it, the decision was made to escort Rebekah to Daamin's office after the meal.

"Take him a plate," Muriel said, placing a container in her hand. "The smell will remind him of his Mama and make him not so mad that you waited so long to speak. Oh, and that you ran away in the first place."

"I didn't even know you knew they slept together," Asiane muttered.

Muriel snorted, and ushered them out of the house. Asiane was driving because now that Muriel considered Rebekah a member of the family- and she was told her status was permanent whether Daamin liked it or not- she was now entitled to security.

"We will tell you about our family troubles soon," the matriarch said. "But for now, talk to Daamin."

They drove back to the area where the club was, and past the coffee shop. Rebekah stirred. "I kinda want to talk to him on my own with no pressure from his family."

Asiane glanced at her and nodded, pulling over. She pointed. "That building there. I'll go do some paperwork at the club. Give me your cell, I'll put my number in and you can call me if you need me. Males can be irrational, so who knows if he will be happy or storm off?"

Rebekah dithered, gathering her nerves, and backtracked towards the cafe where she'd met Daamin before. Ordered herself a strong coffee to give her hands something to do and her eyes something to look at, and started down the block at a brisk pace. It was then that it occurred to her that Daamin's office was in the same vicinity that the Chemical Confectionist had indicated his office was in. The coincidence was almost too astounding to be a fluke.

Blood beginning to boil... Gwenafar's insistence that the arranged mate would be oh so perfect... the groom's ready change of mind to go ahead with the mating... did he know she was pregnant? And if the erstwhile internet personality and Daamin and her future mate were the same person, why hadn't he said something?

God*damn*it.

"Don't jump to conclusions, girl," she muttered to herself. "It's been nine years since you've been arrested for smacking the shit out of someone."

The screech of wheels grabbed her attention, causing her to jerk her coffee. She swore as hot liquid sloshed over her hand and whipped her head around to let loose a string of cusses at the non-driver when a dark blue minivan jerked to a halt and a male jumped out.

And ran right towards her.

***

"Rebekah is coming," Asiane said.

"What?"

"She was posted up outside the house- waiting for you, I guess. Well, Mama fed her-

"Of course."

"-and ordered me to escort her to you to hash out your unfinished business."

Daamin ran his tongue along his teeth. "How's her mood?"

A strange silence on the other end of the line. "You'll see. And Daamin? Be nice. She should be there in five."

His sister's tone of voice put his senses on alert. Asiane knew something she wasn't telling him. The blend of mirth and worry warned him. Daamin sat in his office for all of two minutes before leaving to go to the lobby. They were in between filmings right now and there was no way he'd be able to work on edits while waiting for his future mate.

He reached the entrance and stepped out of the door, deciding to just meet her on her walk, when he heard a female scream.

***

Rebekah screamed when the male grabbed her, and threw her coffee in his face. Screamed more because it was a solid defensive strategy designed to attract attention, because she knew there was a chance Daamin might hear her even if he wasn't expecting her and come investigate, and because her voice in the assailant's ear would just plain hurt.

She took off toward the converted warehouse at a dead run, using the few seconds of the male's distraction to get a head start. He'd catch her, of course, if he wasn't human. But any time she could buy could be the difference between freedom and whatever the kidnapper had planned.

"Daamin!" she hollered at the top of her breath just as she was tackled from behind. Of course, the incident with the twins went through her mind, but only long enough for the memory to just skim her consciousness- she was too busy trying to keep from getting hauled off.

Cruel hands jerked her off her feet. She aimed her nails at the vulnerable parts of his face as a deafening roar announced the presence of a shifter.

Daamin.

The male holding her cursed viciously, as a night black Bear tore down the street, his weight sending shocks through the pavement. Rebekah was flung away and the male turned, trying to flee, but Daamin was on him.

"Don't kill him!" she yelled.

The Bear stood on its hind legs, human in its claws, and threw the male against a nearby building. The male slumped to the ground, head cracking against the pavement and the van screeched away, tires leaving tracks. The Bear stalked his prey, fangs bared in glistening menace. Rebekah pushed to her feet, clutching her side as a cramp clenched her uterus. "Daamin, forget that, I need to sit."

She stumbled to the curb, needing to sit down now. Minutes later a male crouched at her side, wrapping an arm around her back and another under her knees, lifting.

"Are you hurt?" he demanded.

"Not really- at least I don't think so." The cramp was gone and everything felt... normal.

"I'll call an ambulance." His strides crossed ground in record-breaking time. She felt like she was in a slow-moving car, he moved so fast.

"No, just bring Asiane."

Inside the studio, Daamin found her a couch and set her down, an employee appearing a little later with a blanket and another hot drink. The man introduced himself as Logan. "Daamin told me what happened. You okay?"

"I'm fine. Is Asiane coming?"

"He was on the phone with her. He won't let us call the police."

Rebekah nodded, mouth tight. She didn't think he would. If this was Den business, human police couldn't become involved anyway.

Daamin entered the room a moment later, clad only in jeans, not even buttoned, feet bare. He sat on the couch and gathered her into his arms.

"You're naked," she said against his chest.

He said nothing, arms tightening.

Rebekah looked up. "Daamin-"

"Don't speak. I'm very angry. Just... don't say anything."

She began to glance away and a hand clamped around the back of her neck. He swore in Arabic, then switched to English in the middle of the rant. "Never again, do you understand?"

Her temper spiked. "Don't you yell at me. You-"

He kissed her, probably trying to shut her up, except the kiss was as if he was trying to breathe in her soul and brand her as his at the same time. His body hard underneath her lap, his arm a vice around her body. When he pulled away, none of the anger was gone, but it was tempered. Or temporarily soothed.

Daamin refused to let her go back to her hotel. Asiane glanced at her a few times and when they entered the house the girls were already in bed. Daamin took her up the stairs to his room.

Pitiless eyes looked at her. "Strip."

She glanced around the room, ignoring him. Thick carpet, a wooden headboard, and an antique dresser with intricate carving. The place was immaculate.

"Does your mother clean your room?"

He crossed his arms. "My mother hasn't cleaned my room since I was nineteen."

She wasn't sure she believed that, but shrugged.

"Strip."

"I'm not hurt, I think I just pulled a muscle when he tackled me."

Daamin's eyes closed, a growl in his chest. "My enemies know your face. You can't leave me again."

She sat down on the edge of the bed. A colorful quilt was spread atop it, in rich colors that spoke of a faraway homeland.

"Speaking of leaving you again." She pinned him with a steely look. "Are you the Chemical Confectionist?"

His brow rose, arms loosening to his sides as he approached, bending so his face was level with hers. "Is your grandmother Gwenafar Conroy?"

They stared at each other. "This feels a little anticlimactic," she said finally. "Where is all the screaming, the melodrama? You're the male she's been arranging for me, aren't you?"

He straightened, wariness flicking through his eyes. "Do you want me to be?"

"That was like an admission. Not too slick, ace." She scowled at him, heart beating. "Why didn't you say anything? You don't have to mate me if you don't want to."

Daamin laughed. Rebekah's first instinct was to slap him, but she restrained herself out of respect for Muriel.

"You are a silly female. I've been waiting for you to come to your senses and choose me over duty." He stared down at her, arrogant, then paused. "But... I also wanted you to choose duty over personal feelings." He grimaced. "I'm too old to be this confused."

Rebekah rose, closed the gap between them and wrapped her arms around his neck. "Sounds like you have some conflicting goals."

He sighed, and lowered his head the inch he needed in order to take her lips in a kiss.

It was sweet at first, and then the banked heat between them erupted. His hands fisted in her hair as he pushed her onto the bed.

"If you don't want me to fuck you, leave now," he said, voice harsh. "I've been dreaming of you since you left."

She twined her legs around his waist. "Take me."

And he did.

***

Rebekah pressed a hand against her stomach, unsure if the queasiness was nerves or the baby.

They'd wrapped the special episode less than an hour ago and then every hand in the studio rushed to clear the set and prepare it for a mating ceremony.

"Not traditional at all," Gwenafar had grumped. "It should be done properly, in the forest under the sky."

"We're both studio people," Rebekah said. "This is normal for us."

"And cupcakes instead of a cake." Gwenafar had shook her head and smiled. "Just like you. A little odd, but very sweet. It's just as well, I suppose. I have my eye on Amberley for one of my males, and this way she'll get a little exposure, hmm? Let's invite her to the family party, too."

And after the ceremony the Den would retire to Liam's place for a special Solstice party. The human employees didn't celebrate their Christmas for a few more days, so the timing worked out perfectly.

Rebekah retired to a room set aside for her. Muriel, Meredith and all the females of her family already waited, several sets of impatient eyes pinning her when she entered.

"Finally!" Meredith exclaimed. "Hair and makeup!"

"Move your ass, girl," Tamar said.

They descended on her. Muriel held a swath of deep red velvet in her hands, heavily embroidered in black and gold, tiny beads winking in the light.

"This was my mating gown," Daamin's mother said, holding herself with perfect posture, eyes inscrutable. "Your honored mother has given me permission to ask you to wear it."

Rebekah's breath caught as Muriel and Asiane spread the piece of the gown across a couch. A thigh-length tunic with slits up the side and floor-length skirt in full, flowing pleats. A third piece, a swath of heavy fabric that looked like a giant rectangular scarf completed the ensemble.

"It's my favorite color," Rebekah said. "I would love to wear it."

Meredith, at Rebekah's side, wrapped an arm around her daughter's waist, and squeezed. "I told Muriel it was perfect. You aren't a white wedding kind of bride."

"Definitely not," Rebekah said.

They helped her into the gown. It fit perfectly, so either the design was such to accommodate different figures, or they'd had alterations done. Talia and Faridah ushered her towards a chair and knelt, removing her flats. Her hands and feet were cleansed and then pots of maroon paint emerged from a drawer.

"We don't have time for a proper job," Talia said. "But this will do. Must get you mated before you start showing."

And then every pair of Jaafir eyes turned towards her. "When are you telling him?" Asiane asked.

"I really didn't think a bunch of girls could keep a secret so long," Rebekah said without thinking, then winced. Okay, a little sexism there, but still.

Talia rolled her eyes, but said nothing, intent on her work.

"I'll tell him after the ceremony," Rebekah said. "He

told me he didn't want any cubs with a female he wasn't mated to."

"OMG," Faridah said. "What a moron."

"He didn't mean it in a mean way. He was just being responsible."

Muriel patted her hand. "Of course he was, daughter. He will be very pleased."

Tamar did her hair and makeup- Meredith was hopeless with anything more complicated than lip gloss and mascara.

When she stood and looked at herself in the mirror, she recognized the face and body... but the Rebekah in the mirror gleamed. There was an extra layer of mystique and feminine wile she didn't possess on her own.

"I look beautiful," she said, lips curling in a smug fashion.

"Daamin will praise god he is so lucky," Asiane said. "In order to make allies, he told me he would have accepted a-"

Rebekah held up a hand. "No body shaming, please. Short, tall, plump, warty- I'm sure his mate would have been lovely."

Asiane rolled her eyes. "Right."

Rebekah inhaled, let out the breath slowly. "Alright. I'm ready."

Outside the set had been turned into an indoor winter wonderland. Delicate arches of white, with boughs of evergreen, holly, and red berries woven through swaths of sheer white fabrics hung strategically from the ceiling to form a tent-like structure. Tall silver candle stands and fat white candles. Rebekah realized her dress would stand out starkly, bringing the eye to her as a focal point.

"Is that a snow machine?" Rebekah asked.

Meredith chuckled. "Yup. It's going to look fabulous on camera." Her adopted mother took her arm and escorted her to her waiting mate. There was no formal march, and no music- it wasn't the Bear way. Family and friends and co-workers stood in a loose circle, Gwenafar and Daamin waiting on a slightly raised dais.

Daamin turned his head, eyes flaring when he saw her. He left the dais, striding towards her, contained energy and predator intensity. When he reached her, hands wrapped around her waist and lifted her with effortless strength high into the air. She clutched his shoulders, laughing, the veil covering over her head and folds of her skirt flowing around him.

"You are the most beautiful thing I have seen," he said. "The males of my Clan would fall at your feet and Challenge me for the right to court you."

"Let's hope it doesn't come to that," she said, voice dry. "So the sooner we get hitched, the better."

He lowered her slowly, a small smile on his lips, head lowering so he could brush a kiss on her earlobe. "Yes," he crooned. "The ceremony, and then more mating."

***

There was a raucous reception/holiday party after the ceremony. She and her new husband found a quiet corner where they could watch the proceedings quietly, and just hold hands. They'd spent too many weeks apart and the chance to just touch and sit was priceless.

"Do you think we're bonding?" Rebekah asked, her head on his shoulder.

"Possibly," Daamin said, voice deep. "I've seen plenty of matebonds that take time to develop." He nudged her chin so she raised her head for a kiss. When he pulled away, eyes glowing, he said, "But even if we are not true mates, you are still my wife. And you will always be my wife. *Mine.*"

The last word was said with such fierceness Rebekah didn't doubt him. She'd also seen the kind of matebonds that weren't bursts of lightning, but slow and gentle. So she was happy to wait and let nature take its course. For now, it was enough that she loved her husband.

Her breath caught.

"What is it?" he asked.

"I just realized I love you."

"Is that all?"

Rebekah snarled, straightening enough to aim a solid punch at his chest. He laughed. "I've known for weeks that I loved you." He paused, expression bemused. "After only two days."

Her eyes narrowed. "Hey, ever heard of love at first sight?"

He smiled, and kissed her again. Heat crawled between them, an aching desire that stole her breath.

"Get a room," someone yelled, not entirely coherent.

Rebekah sighed and pulled away, gazing around the room. Her eyes caught on the buffet spread, hosted by Daamin's company. Talia was sneaking towards a punch bowl.

"I think your sister is spiking the punch with booze," Rebekah said.

Daamin laughed. "It's probably the shifter stuff, too."

"Are you going to stop her?"

He shrugged. "It's a party."

See, that was why she liked him, and his family.

Asiane strolled towards them, stripping a cupcake of its wrapper with quick, efficient movements. "This is my fourth," she said. "These things are damn good."

"You could try and have a ladies night at the bar once a month," Rebekah suggested. "Girls only, have male strippers and a cupcake bar. Amberley would give you a good deal."

Asiane's lips pursed. "Beefcake & Cupcakes. That's not a bad idea."

Daamin sighed, pressing a kiss on Rebekah's forehead. Rebekah looked for Amberley in the crowd, and caught the baker's eyes as she brought in a fresh tray of cupcakes to the dessert table. Rebekah waved her over. Amberley paused to give instructions to an assistant and then trotted over.

"Is everything okay?" Amberley asked, expression anxious.

"The cupcakes are wonderful." Rebekah grinned at her. "My sister-in-law wants to talk business."

"Let's go outside," Asiane suggested. "I need some fresh air, anyway."

The two women left together and Rebekah took a deep breath, taking Daamin's hand.

"Daamin, I have to tell you something."

He stilled, hand tightening around hers. "Yes."

The careful tone of his voice worried her. What did he think she was about to say? Though she supposed she couldn't blame him since even she could hear the fine, nervous tremble in her voice.

She face stiffened. "I wanted it to be like mating present. And it wasn't on purpose, it was more of a surprise present, and I hope you're not-"

"Rebekah." His deep voice was edged, shading into dark.

"I'm pregnant."

She stared in his eyes, seeing the shock that slid through the endless pools of brown. Hid lids closed. One breath, two, and when she would have pulled away, heart breaking, his eyes opened again. And their expression...

He cupped her cheek with his hand. "Are you well?" he asked with quiet joy.

She nodded, blinking several times. "Yeah."

He gathered her close. "This is indeed a wonderful Solstice present." A hand over her hair, the gentleness of the stroke touching her to the core. "We must make sure you're protected. I have enemies."

"Clan Conroy will help," she said. "If you say the cub is in danger- they will help. We need our cubs."

He rose, pulling her with him. "That is for another time. Today I only want to celebrate."

Daamin pulled her into his arms, head lowering for another kiss when a roar and a woman's scream rent through the air. He stiffened, met Rebekah's eyes for one searing second and they both turned and ran, bursting out of the side door of the studio and into the brightly lit lot. Sprinkles of snow fell in the orange light, creating an ethereal effect.

"Amberley!" Rebekah saw the woman on the ground, crumpled, and tried to run to her.

Daamin growled at her. "Get inside."

She snarled back, swiping at him with her nails. "She's my friend."

He let her go after a hard look, matching her pace. Rebekah was at the baker's side in a few seconds, kneeling. "Amberley?"

Amberley moaned, a low sound, and her eyelids fluttered open. "I'm just stunned. They took Asiane. Asiane was kidnapped."

Bear in Furry Armor

A Clan Conroy Novella

1

Amberley stood in front of the espresso machine, glancing over her shoulder at the shop's glass door. It was still dark, she'd just flipped the sign to open. Customers weren't expected for at least another fifteen minutes.

Facing the recalcitrant box of worthless metal squarely, an evil little smile curling her lips, she lifted her finger and crooned.

"Opus, non refert Apparatus."

A jolt of energy and it sparked to life, began brewing. These small magics didn't require the preparation of spellwork, being mostly bits of focused will powered by her innate talent. Satisfied, she inhaled the scent of a light Colombian roast that filled the air. She turned her back, prepared to focus her attention on filling the case with freshly baked scones, when the machine sputtered to death again.

She whirled, lifted an ankle to kick it, and pointed her finger.

"Interrogabo vos et ego ceruisam!"

"I don't know if the coffee machine speaks Latin, Stormy."

Amberley stifled a shriek, whirling around with her fingers hastily tucked into her pocket, free hand covering her heart to still the rapid, startled beat.

"Jayson!" She stared at the tall, sandy-haired Bear who'd haunted her since senior high.

Stalked her in her dreams with his slow drawl and wicked dark eyes, the way his sandy hair fell over his forehead as if waiting for the right woman to come along and… oh, joy. She couldn't think those thoughts. Her mother would hex the man, for sure. Only a warlock would do for Laticia's only daughter. Or so Amberley had been told since puberty.

"I didn't hear the door chime," she said. Nor had she felt the blast of cool, early winter air that should have accompanied him entering her shop.

He leaned on the counter, a little grin on his lips. He nodded at the machine. "Giving you trouble, Stormy? I might be able to help with that."

Amberley gritted her teeth. She didn't know why the nickname amused him, or why he called her Stormy. She was perfectly polite in public.

"Help how?"

"Well, I may know a thing or two about small appliances, if you've ever asked around."

She knew he fixed stuff for a living. She'd seen him landscaping, painting houses, repairing cars. No one was quite sure exactly what his one-man business specialized in other than being the man all the single ladies, and ladies with inept husbands, went to when they needed a strong man to help with something... and the view he provided in the summer probably helped his popularity as well.

"Do you clean pools?" Amberley asked, then blushed.

His brow quirked, and he grinned, leaning on the counter even further. "Did you need a pool boy, ma'am?"

Amberley cleared her throat. "Excuse me. I didn't mean to say that aloud."

He nodded to the coffee machine again. "Want me to take a look at it? Or were you just going to wiggle your fingers again?"

"Wiggle my... whatever are you talking about, Jayson Conroy?" She refused to meet his eyes.

He snorted, then proceeded to walk behind her counter. "You can play innocent with me, Stormy, if it makes you happy. Just keep your finger in your pocket."

"What do you know about my finger?" The question came out a bit sharper than she might have liked. Mother always said to keep your voice low, modulated. Otherwise, people would know they'd rattled you. She cleared her throat. "Excuse me. Why do you mention my finger?"

"Hush," he said, absently, fiddling with the machine. "I know this brand. They had a recall. Alpha had some issues with his, too. Expensive scrap metal."

She stared at it with dislike. "My mother talked me into it."

"Well, the idea was right, just not the execution. You still have the box?"

"Yes. But I bought it from Best Buy."

He grimaced. "That's a damn shame. Worst return policy in the business. Tell you what, there's a used restaurant supply store up in Tacoma. I'm headed that way this week, I'll nose around for you."

She folded her arms. "And what do you want in return for such a favor, Jayson Conroy?"

Jayson turned and faced her, hooking a thumb in his belt. Broad shoulders relaxed, liquid brown eyes wide. Innocent. As innocent as her mother's 'herb' garden. The one you touched at your own peril.

"How about a tour of the kitchen? I have this powerful desire to see how cupcakes are baked."

"That's the silliest…"

"Are you calling me silly?" He stepped forward, thumb leaving his belt, and mock glowered. "There's a consequence for being disrespectful to a male."

She wanted to roll her eyes, but it would be rude. Jayson was playing with her, but she wasn't exactly sure why. Or why now, anyway.

"Unlike you, I don't believe I've called you anything other than your given name."

He tapped the tip of her nose. "You like when I call you Stormy, don't you though? No one else knows you have a hurricane inside you. They all think you're this quiet little thing, but I know better."

She drew back, eyes narrowed, and pushed back her flicker of temper, the tip of her finger sparking.

"And how in the Solstice Moon do you think you know me so well?"

He lowered his head, lips close to her ear. Not close

enough to imply she wasn't a lady… but still closer than was proper for a man not her boyfriend.

"Because I watch you, Stormy. I've been watching you for a long time."

Amberley took a step backward, sniffing, ignoring the fact that he probably heard how her heart skipped a few beats. Thrice darned Bears. "I guess that makes you a stalker."

"Or a male who sees something he likes."

She held his eyes. True, she was known as being a polite, friendly, non-confrontational person. Because she'd worked very hard to be known as that, thanks very much. But she could stand up for herself when it was needed.

"For a male who sees something he likes, he sure has taken his time in saying anything about it."

His eyes narrowed and Amberley realized her runaway mouth had implied… something. Something she'd rather keep to herself.

He closed the step between them. "Well, now. We've both been busy. Are you saying you want me to say something?"

"My mother would hex a fit," she said, then snapped her mouth shut.

Jayson smiled slyly. "Am I the only one in town who's guessed your family secret, Stormy?"

Oh… joy. "Would you like to tour the kitchen now?" she asked, voice bright. "I think I smell the batch of scones I just put in. And there's a new lemondrop cupcake I was going to taste test today as well."

He allowed her to move towards the kitchen door. "I wouldn't mind a lemondrop. I like a little sour with my sweet."

Amberley hurried through the doors, not waiting to see if he accompanied her. Inside the kitchen, the scent of blueberries, cinnamon and the little hard lemon candies she crushed for decorations on the rim of the lemondrop cupcakes soothed her temper. She approached a pan of frosted confections, thankful she'd already worked the tiny magic on the batter that would make them actually taste good.

No one but her mother knew she couldn't bake worth a tarnished dime. But a little well-meaning moon magic always went a long way. She picked up one of the cupcakes and peeled back the wrapper, biting cautiously into the cake, and winced. A little dry.

Glancing over her shoulder as Jayson entered the kitchen, she casually rested her hand on the counter next to the tray of treats. Her finger stiffened, and she opened her mouth to-

"Uh, Stormy, no cheating," he said, grabbing her wrist.

"Fu-udge," she said, as her hand went numb from the reabsorbed energy. "Jayson, what are you doing?"

"Give me one to taste without all the extra fairy dust."

He spoke too close to her ear, breath on her neck. Her lower body clenched. She turned, glaring at him, and yanked her hand away. The traitorous energy spilled out of her finger and sparked, aimed directly at him. Her eyes widened in sudden panic.

"Oh, sugar honey…"

He blinked, staring. "Are you trying to witch me?"

"No! No, I would never-" she paused, cleared her throat. "Um… there is no such thing as witches."

Jayson laughed, reaching around her to snatch one of the cupcakes. The rims of his irises glowed pink for just a

second. Amberley winced.

He peeled away the wrapper and sank strong white teeth into the cake. Chewed. Amberley gnawed at her bottom lip.

"It's a new batter," she said. "Umm… I think the proportions are wrong."

"Well." He chewed a few more seconds. "I taste the lemon."

That was something anyway, since she wasn't even sure it was lemon she'd flavored them with, having a tendency to… mistake the bottles. But she loved to bake, and she loved sweets, so even if she still had some learning to do, she just couldn't give up her shop. It was the only thing she'd ever done on her own, without her mother… helping.

Jayson swallowed. Visibly. "Stormy, have you ever thought of taking a few classes at the community college? Then you wouldn't need to…" he wiggled his fingers.

Amberley glared. "I'm sure I have no idea what you're talking about." She sniffed. "Mrs. Nelson taught me to bake."

"That's the problem," he muttered. "The squirrels never tried to swipe her apple pies."

She crossed her arms, tucking her hands carefully under her armpits, out of temptation's way. "And I guess you think the proper thing for me to do is go open up a little used book store and sell tarot cards," she said, fuming. "And find a nice warlock and settle down-"

"Well, I don't know about the warlock bit, but if your aim is to settle down, I know a Bear who may be interested."

Her mouth closed. They stared at each other. His eyes

were still amused, still brown with a bit of pink. But his mouth was firm, no playful quirk of the lips- and Jayson Conroy always had a smile on his face.

Except when he was conducting serious business.

Amberley licked her lips, watching as he followed the movement. The rim of pink deepened to fuchsia and he leaned forward.

Oh, moon. She wanted him to kiss her. But not like this. "Jayson," she whispered, "before you kiss me, I think you should know I accidentally got you with some of the… fairy dust."

"I know," he whispered back. "It's okay, Stormy. You can't witch me when I've been bewitched since eleventh grade."

And while she was sorting through the moon-blessed implications in that statement, his soft lips closed over hers, and there was no room left to think. At all.

2

Her lips were as sweet as he'd imagined. The lemon on their tongues mingled, hers softened by a bit of sugar and the blueberries she'd been munching on while baking. And a unique blend of flavors that was all Amberley. Warm, soft female, her hair scented with the crackle of thunder and sweetness of rain. Skin the soft heat of a summer day. All female, all witch.

And she thought he didn't know.

Jayson slid an arm around her waist, pulling her against his chest, careful to entrap her arms. Didn't need her hexing him on accident because he'd startled her. The town still floated with tales of lesser males who'd tried to sneak a kiss out of Amberley Levinson and gotten blue lips and even bluer cocks in return. Though the cock part was usually only discovered when it was time to change for PE.

They were eight plus years past all that, and in that time, he'd kept his distance. Her Mama was no joke, and he was busy building up a living anyway. A male had no business taking a mate and having cubs when he had nothing to take care of them with. But he was settled now, and Amberley was still single. Still watching him with inscrutable, rain-cloud eyes when she thought he wasn't looking.

He was always looking.

"Jayson," she sighed against his mouth.

He pulled away when his fangs began to itch. That was always the signal to back up, get ahold of himself. It wasn't quite time for Bear to waken, to stake a Claim. It hurt, though. His hands ached to cup her sweet, round bottom. His cock hardened, and for a few blissful moments he imagined lifting her up on that counter, wrapping her legs around his waist and sinking inside her, fucking her while she mewled his name. But not yet.

He had to deal with Laticia Levinson first.

A tinkle of bells in the front of the shop gave him the incentive to step back. "I think that's a customer, Stormy."

Her eyes widened and she pulled away, hurrying past him without another word.

He left a few moments later, when he was certain his body was behaving itself. No need for anyone to know- yet- where his interests lay. Jayson opened the kitchen door and stepped out only to see Gwenafar Conroy, elder of the Clan from which he took his surname, seat herself at a round window side table, a pink rectangular box in her hand.

Her head turned immediately, sharp eyes moving from his face to Amberley's.

"Jayson, good morning," the Mother's Council Elder said. "Is everything all right with your equipment, Amberley?"

"I was having some trouble with the coffee machine," Amberley said, as he opened his mouth to reply.

He filched a recycled paper cup, pouring himself a healthy sixteen ounces since that was what he'd come for in the second place- first place had just been the urge to see her. Gwenafar Conroy opened her box, taking her time to choose a cupcake. He sipped his coffee, certain the treat the Alpha's mother put in her mouth would taste magical.

He snorted.

"Something funny?" Amberley asked, voice tight.

"Not at all, Stormy. I'll call you when I'm on my way to Tacoma."

"Thanks," she muttered. "Have a cupcake."

He waited until she fled into her kitchen again and turned his attention back to Gwenafar, considering. She'd be a powerful ally to have in order to win Laticia over- or simply subdue her. And he knew for certain that if he expressed interest in the human Amberley, Gwenafar would consider it her Motherly duty to interfere to get things rolling.

"She's a nice girl," he said, moving from behind the counter.

"A talented baker."

"You'd be surprised."

Blue eyes regarded him. "And friends with my granddaughter."

"Rebekah? Yeah." He didn't take a seat, but he paused next to her table before leaving. "She's unmated, too. Amberley, I mean."

And now he had Gwenafar's full attention. "That's very true. A shame, really. A lovely, successful businessperson, but no mate."

"I'd stake a Claim, but I don't think her mother likes

shifters. And you know how those Levinson's are..." He wiggled his free hand.

Gwenafar's lips pursed. "Laticia Levinson doesn't frighten me. But if I knew a Bear who had honorable intentions towards Amberley, I'd be happy to help smooth things along. A New Year's mating ceremony would be lovely."

He smiled at the Alpha's mother. "I like New Year's."

She returned his smile. "I'm so happy to hear it."

***

He waited until Monday, the day he knew Amberley would be closed for business, and called her up. His pickup idled across from her house, smoke wafting down the street in the early morning chill.

"How did you get my cell number, Jayson Conroy?"

He loved how her voice shaded from Sunday school sweet to vixen sharp in the course of nine words.

"I called the shop, it forwarded to your cell."

A pause on the other side of the line. "Oh. Well. How can I help you?"

He smiled. "Well, I'm headed to Tacoma to the supply store I told you about and it occurred to me I don't know what I'm looking for. You should come along, Stormy. We'll have lunch while we're there."

"Are you inviting me out on a business date?"

"Well, I wouldn't go so far as the business part. How soon can you be ready? You don't need to do any of that girly primping stuff."

She snorted. "I'll thank you not to instruct me on my morning regime. Thirty minutes?"

"I'm right outside waiting for you. No rush, though."

"What?"

Jayson watched as the blinds of her living room window rattled, opening a sliver. He lifted a finger and waved.

"I've got coffee waiting for you. And not the gas station kind. Get dressed, female."

He disconnected, and sat his seat back a bit, knowing it would take at least thirty minutes.

It would be a welcome thirty minutes, since he'd gotten up long before dawn in order to finish his morning job. He'd contracted with the city to plow snow once it hit, and had a crew under him ready to work, but this morning had been spent on maintenance, making sure the winter fleet was ready to go come the first bite of real cold weather.

His cell rang, and Jayson answered when he saw who it was. "Alpha."

"My mother says you're courting that human girl."

Jayson was sure she'd said a whole lot more than that. "Yeah. Amberley Levinson."

A pause on the other end. "Isn't that family...?"

"The mother is a bit of a doozy, but Stormy doesn't have a mean... well. She handles herself well."

"Make sure you're sure," Liam warned. "I can head my mother off now, but if too much time goes by, she'll have your ceremony planned and names picked out for the cubs."

Jayson laughed. "I have my own names picked out, thanks, though I'm sure Stormy will have something to say about it."

Liam grunted. "Like that, huh? Good Bear. You're at a good age to settle down. Business doing well?"

"Yes, sir. I've got some money put aside. I'm taking her to Tacoma today to find some equipment for her place."

"Good. That's good. Female should have the use of something besides your cock. You call me if you need anything."

Jayson disconnected, suppressing the urge to whistle. His Alpha approved, which was a bonus. He would Claim Stormy even if Liam was against it, but this was much better.

He was surprised when Amberley exited her door in less than ten minutes, eyes bright and cheeks pink, a smug smile on her lips. She trotted down her walkway, a medium height sprite in jeans too tight to be legal, on oversized pink plaid shirt, long mink brown hair rich against the white of her quilted vest. Her lips were shiny, and he could tell she'd slathered some of that stuff on her eyelashes.

She didn't look a day over eighteen.

"I told you it wouldn't take thirty minutes," she said, opening the passenger door and climbing in. "But you'd already hung up."

"I'm impressed."

She sniffed, eyeing the untouched coffee cup in the holder, the little plastic green thingy still in the lid.

"Go on, have your coffee," he said, and reached for the little brown bag on the dash. "Scone, too. I thought you'd like one you didn't bake."

She slanted him a look, as if to check for mockery, but his conscience was clear.

"Thank you, sir," she said, and took a bite of the scone, washing it down with coffee. "Oh, that's the good stuff."

"I wasn't sure how you take it, so I just did the regular splash of milk and two packets of sugar."

"This is just fine, thank you."

Pleased he'd been able to feed her, he put the truck in gear and drove off. "We'll have a proper lunch in Tacoma. Do witches eat like shifters?"

"There is no such thing as witches."

Her response lacked any true conviction, so he decided not to call her out for a lie. Shifters knew all about witches and even humans had a damn good idea- why the Covens liked to pretend they didn't exist, he'd never know.

"Why are you grinning?" Amberley asked, grey eyes suspicious. She eyed her cup.

Alone, in a truck, with Amberley Levinson for the entire trip to Tacoma and back. "I have you all to myself. And it's only taken eight years."

3

Amberley wasn't sure how life was just plodding along one day, and then the next Jayson Conroy was in her shop sending out all kinds of smoke signals. It was as if the Fates had simply pressed the go button.

She frowned, wondering if her mother was playing around with love potions again. She'd been hinting about grandkids, but Amberley was certain Mother hadn't been trying to attract a Bear.

"Why the frown, Stormy?"

"Just thinking."

"Hmm. Should I be worried?"

"Why? Because women who think are dangerous?"

His eyes widened, and he glanced at her. "Females are dangerous, period. Just, for one moment, consider Gwenafar Conroy." He paused. "And your mother."

Amberley considered. "Point taken." If she was Bear, and male, she'd be a little afraid of Liam's mom, too. "So what's the trip for today? I mean, I'm tagging along, but you had planned it already."

"Picking up some bags of salt for the winter. They don't have the wholesale quantity I need at home."

Made sense. It was such a tiny town, many small business owners drove into Tacoma or Seattle to gather bulk supplies they didn't want to pay shipping and handling fees for.

"Do you have the city contracts for snow removal this year?"

"Yup."

"Your crew did a good job last year."

"Thanks."

Her fingers tapped her thigh. Was she going to have to make small talk the whole way? With him sending her those little glances like she was a cherry-filled pastry and he a starving man?

"Turn the radio on, Stormy," he said, voice soft. "Relax."

Amberley realized that not only was her back stiff, but that he'd be able to sense her tension. He was a shifter, after all. She fiddled with the radio until it was on her favorite classical station, ignored his sigh, and settled back to listen to the Sunday morning opera.

***

They took care of business first, loading up his truck with bags of salt from the supply store- and he'd argued with her about that.

"What are you doing?" he asked, when she bent down

to lift a fifty-pound bag.

She frowned at him. "What does it look like?"

The damn thing was heavy. She was athletic enough, she supposed, but the weight of the bag was distributed in a way that made it-

"Amberley, put that down."

She glanced at him, a little surprised to see heat in eyes to match his almost snarly tone.

Amberley straightened from her crouch. "Are you telling me you're one of those Bears?"

He paused, opened his mouth, and closed it. Then folded his arms. "What Bears?"

"The kind of Bear who thinks the little female shouldn't lift anything heavier than a casserole dish."

"It's not that you're incapable of lifting heavy objects, Amberley," he said in an oh-so-reasonable voice. "I just don't want anyone to think I make my female work for me."

"Your female? And why in the blessed moon would you care what other people think? Besides-" she crouched back down, made sure her back was properly aligned and got her arms under the bag and lifted. "Not heavy. See?"

He stared at her, face set. "You should put that down before you hurt yourself."

She sniffed. "You should stop wasting time and start lifting."

Amberley walked past him to the open truck bed, heaved the bag inside, and turned, brushing her hands.

He hauled one bag, then another over his shoulder, back to her. She admired how his faded dark wash jeans hugged a toned rear, and almost didn't hear his mutter.

"Never should have given females the vote. Now they think they can lift stuff."

"What?"

"I didn't say anything."

The next stop was the restaurant depot, where Amberley chose a quality used machine to replace the one on recall. She was pleased- it was a better model and for a lower price.

"I don't know why I never thought of buying used before," she said. "Mother insists on everything being new, no energy signatures... uh, new."

He tugged a lock of her hair. "Yeah. Ready for lunch?"

Amberley wasn't sure of the too casual tone in his voice, but nodded warily. He was up to something, she just wasn't sure what. She knew it wasn't malicious- Jayson Conroy didn't have a mean bone in his body, except for that one time he nearly beat a boy silly. But the boy had deserved it, trying to take advantage of a cheerleader. It was the last tailgate party she ever went to, after her mother got wind of that fiasco. Fortunately, he was well enough liked that Alpha Liam had been able to smooth things over... especially since there were witnesses to the attempted assault.

When they turned into a section of town Amberley recognized, she knew what was up.

"Jayson Conroy, exactly where are you taking me for lunch?"

He pulled up to a little cafe bookstore, parking. "You mentioned your mother wanted you to open one of these, I thought it might be fun to-"

"This is a Coven-run establishment."

Chocolate eyes widened. "What?" He turned his head

towards the café, expression enthusiastic. "How interesting."

He hopped out before she could say another word, moving pretty blessed fast when he wanted, and had her door open, ushering her out of the truck while talking briskly. As if he thought he could just talk over her objections and she wouldn't notice.

Amberley dug her heels in at the front door. "Jayson."

He faced her. "Stormy."

"Why are we having lunch here?"

The store did a brisk little business in organic and vegan sandwiches; salads and smoothies blended with special concoctions. The kinds of concoctions her mother liked to whip up in the kitchen.

"I wanted to help you get in touch with your heritage."

She folded her arms, stepping out of the way as a customer exited the store giving Amberley and Jayson a glance. "You just think you're funny."

He considered it, then nodded. "I think I am pretty funny. So... wanna get our fortunes told over a turkey pesto panini?"

Amberley sighed and entered the store. She was hungry, and it would be rude to refuse his choice when he was treating. And if the atmosphere of the little shop felt like home, well then, all the better.

But she braced herself, resigned for the hedgewitch hotline to start rolling when she recognized the red-haired woman standing at the register.

"Blessed Be, Amber, it's been awhile."

"Blessed Be, Ray."

It'd been awhile because the main way her magic weak

family stayed out of the crossfire of Coven politics was to play least in sight. Her mother might daydream about Amberley wedding a rich, powerful Warlock, but the reality was her father wanted them to amalgamate into human society, so in a generation or two they could all but pass for regular. Her mother would have a fit if Amberley dated a shifter, not just because that would definitely not be passing as a plain human, but because shifters weren't considered entirely... human.

"Are you here for a-"

"Just lunch," she said hastily. "The turkey cranberry panini looks good. With a side of kettle chips."

"I'll have the same thing," Jayson said. "What's the pink drink?"

Amberley glared at him. "You don't want the pink drink-"

"It's a strawberry coconut smoothie infused with our own house blend designed to attract your true love," Ray said.

"Is that why it's twenty-five dollars?"

The shifter sounded far too curious for Amberley's liking. "It's just a tourist kind of thing, Jayson. There isn't an actual spell in it. Just a blend of B-vitamins."

He gave her a speculative look, then turned to Ray. "I'll take it. I need all the help I can get."

Ray looked between Amberley and Jayson, blue-green eyes curious. "Anything to drink for you, Amber?"

"Tea. Plain green tea."

"Don't be a spoilsport," he said cheerfully, as they chose a table.

One of the things she'd always liked about him was his

good-natured, laidback personality. Many of the male Bears were moody, broody, growly brawlers. Jayson had fangs well enough, and would use them, but it took real effort to provoke him.

A few summers ago, she'd snuck into the Bear shifter bar off the local highway and sat at a small table in a corner. Karaoke night- she'd watched him at the bar, joking and laughing with his Clan mates. A human had tried to pick a fight and Jayson just ignored him, even though some of the males he was with took exception on Jayson's behalf. He just shrugged it off though. Like he knew his own strength and didn't have to prove it.

"What are you thinking about?" he asked.

She glanced up, realizing she'd been staring at her hands while she thought. "You'd make a good mate, you know. Why aren't you married?"

He stilled, half-smile gone, studying her. "Why do you think I'd make a good mate?"

She tilted her head, returning his attention. "You have an even temper, you work hard. I know you even do some of your jobs at cost for the mothers in town in a financial bind."

"Maybe I'm just trying to get in their pants."

Amberley giggled. It was so funny- Jayson Conroy, the town Bear-in-Furry Armor with not one hint to his name of being bad in a relationship or mistreating a girl.

He leaned an elbow on the table, arching a brow. "You think I'm above trying to get in a female's pants?"

His voice deepened, a sensual croon that cut off her giggle. She inhaled, feeling the tug of attraction between them. Skeins of glowing gold and pink energy tangled around his hands, reaching out to ensnare hers. Threads that hadn't been there even a few days ago.

Amberley inhaled sharply. "What are you doing, Jayson?"

"What do you see?"

"Something I shouldn't see. It wouldn't work with us."

"Because your mother doesn't want you to be with a shifter."

Her eyes narrowed. Ray approached with a tray and sat their orders on the table. They waited until she stepped away before talking again.

"How do you know that?" she asked him.

"I've made it my business to know." He stared at his drink, the beginning of a scowl on his face. "And now that I think about it, I don't know why I waited so long to say something. It always felt like it wasn't the right time, but that doesn't make any damn sense. Almost as if every time I thought about finally telling you how I felt, something stopped me."

Oh, blessed. Don't let him start coming to conclusions that might cause problems for her mother.

"Please think before you make any accusations," she said, voice very quiet.

He met her eyes, and for once his dark irises were grim rather than warm. He held her gaze for a long moment. "I won't accuse her. For you. But I've waited too long to speak, Amberley."

Joy, her name again. Twice in one day.

"I've wanted you since high school. I dated other females a few times, but they weren't what I wanted."

Amberley picked up her sandwich and took a bite. Roasted turkey and cranberry burst on her tongue. She took a sip of her tea.

"And what do you want from me now?"

He touched her cheek, exerting subtle pressure until she looked at him again. "I want to court you. I told Gwenafar."

Amberley choked on her tea. "You... what? That's tantamount to staking a Claim!"

Now a small smile played around his lips. "What does the witch know about Claims?"

If he thought she hadn't been studying him, studying the shifters, then he hadn't been watching her as closely as he said.

"I know enough. I know when you tell Gwenafar Conroy you want to mate, that woman will move heaven and earth to get you mated, wedded, bedded, and pregnant with twins before the girl has time to pick out colors for her ceremony."

He grinned. "Yeah. I sicced her on your Mom."

She stared, appalled. "Oh... Jayson. You didn't."

He finally picked up his sandwich, six feet of smug male, and took a huge bite. "I did. Just wait. She'll do all my work for me, and by the time Gwenafar is done with your mother, I'll look like an angel in comparison."

"There hasn't been a Coven-Clan feud in six generations."

"There won't be one now. Trust me, Stormy."

"And what happens after the courtship?"

Steel in his eyes, heat in the wicked curve of his mouth. "I'm playing the forever game, Amberley. If you want out, say so now."

She took another bite of her sandwich.

4

When they returned to town, Jayson helped her install the machine, and then left. She could tell he wanted to kiss her. The way his broad shoulders slanted, and how he eyed her with a masculine heat in his eyes. But… she needed time to breathe a bit. Everything was happening so fast. One day she was daydreaming about him, and the next day they were… courting.

It was what she'd wanted all along, and now that it was finally happening, she needed to get her balance.

Amberley decided to stay a few extra hours in the shop and work on the flavors of the month. Each time she created a new batch, she tried to do it by hand first. She tried. But she just didn't know what it was, why her proportions were always off or her batters never rose… or what. But each time she wound up having to add just a touch of magic to finally make the batch work.

Nothing that would hurt anyone, of course. There were no compulsions in her cakes, nothing to trick a customer into liking her offerings. Just… the magic fixed whatever problems she was inadvertently causing by hand.

"You shouldn't waste your magic on baking."

Amberley didn't turn, having sensed her mother's presence already. "It's how I make my living, Mother."

Laticia Levinson set her designer handbag on the counter next to Amberley. "We need to talk."

She hated those words. "Yes, I figured a talk was coming."

"Ray called me."

Amberley finished doling out the last scoop of pistachio batter into a silver liner and wiped her hands on a towel. She turned to face her mother.

Laticia Levinson didn't look anything like her daughter. A tall, curvy woman with a mass of ebony sisterlocks, eyes startling hazel against the backdrop of deep brown skin, her curving cheekbones and full lips made her a very handsome woman. Amberley mostly took after her father, though there were hints of her mother in the fullness of her lips and bone structure, but her coloring often confused individuals who weren't used to bi-racial people and didn't understand how tricky genetics could be in determining outward looks.

"Is this about Jayson?"

"Of course." Laticia's mouth tightened. "And it's about how I had Gwenafar Conroy on my porch asking me if I have any objections to a mating between my daughter and a Bear. A Bear, Amberley."

"What's wrong with a Bear, if he treats me right?"

"They are barely even human. And not a bit of magic-"

"Mom, I'm barely even a hedgewitch. In another generation, our family will be so human it won't make much difference."

"Then marry a human," her mother snapped. "Not something that turns into an animal."

Amberley turned away, picking up the tray of cupcakes and taking them to the convection oven. "You know, I never did understand how a woman with your complexion could be such a bigot. You'd think you'd know better."

"I'm not going to argue with you over this. I forbid-"

Amberley turned. "You can't forbid anything. You don't have the magic to forbid anything."

They stared at each other. Amberley took a breath, deliberately dispelling her own tension. "I'm courting Jayson, Mom. I've not met a single man since high school I like any better than him, and he's all but said his intentions are towards marriage. He'll be a kind husband and a good provider and father."

"And your children will be cubs."

"Which means I'll never be cold in the winter. You have to accept it."

"No, I do not. Not until you are fully matebonded and there is no possible chance left to turn you from this path. And you may never be matebonded."

Amberley inhaled, biting back words. "I'm going to do my best to make sure we do bond. Then you won't be able to interfere ever again."

Laticia picked up her purse. "I can see your mind is made up. We'll see how it all plays out."

Amberley watched her mother leave, knowing full well that those words were a declaration of battle and not an admission of defeat.

***

Amberley tracked Jayson down a few hours later.

It was small town and years spent keeping an eye on him gave her a general idea of where she might find him, who his usual clients were. She could have called first, but her own restless energy demanded a hunt instead. Plus, it gave her time to think and calm herself from the mini confrontation with her mother.

The blood thinned with each generation, so Laticia was just a tad stronger, a tad darker than Amberley. She didn't think her mother would hurt her, but Jayson was a different story. They'd have to step carefully, and keep an eye out for... tricks. At least until Amberley figured out how to get her mother on her side.

She pulled up to a medium-sized frame house. Winter was a slow month, but most of the single ladies in town had their holiday lights and decorations hung by Jayson. For one thing, if he fell off a roof it was unlikely he'd break something. And for another, he was fun to watch.

The Bear climbed down the ladder he was on as Amberley approached. He was in a navy thermal shirt and jeans, shifter heat insulating him from the winter chill. There were still a few days to go until the first big snow storm, and she supposed he'd be busy salting the streets then.

"You keep busy," she said.

He slid an arm around her waist and kissed her forehead with the ease as if they were a long-time couple.

"I've got to eat, Stormy," he said, touching her nose. "And it keeps me from getting fat."

As if.

He studied her. "You want to talk about something?"

She nodded at the half-hung lights. "Can you take a break?"

"Yeah. I'm not hourly. Let's go sit in your car, it's still warm and I don't need you catching a chill."

How... wifey.

They settled in the car, Amberley turning the heat up another notch because she hated cold hands, and stared at the steering wheel.

"Come on, baby, what's wrong?"

She glanced at him. "My mother came to see me."

"That must have been an interesting conversation."

"She told me not to see you."

His eyes went flinty. "And what did you tell her?"

Amberley took a deep breath. "I told her we're courting, and that your intentions are of the honorable kind."

Cool fingers on her cheek. Amberley turned her head, meeting his eyes again, now softened to molten chocolate. "So it's official then?"

A thread in his soft voice. Of triumph, of suppressed desire. Whatever it was, it made her shiver. His eyes lowered, tracing the curve of her lips.

"It's official," she said. "We're... going steady."

He smiled, a lazy, thoroughly satisfied expression that might have been cocky on another man. "I think we should seal it with a kiss."

Jayson leaned forward, hand curling around the back of her neck. The first touch of his lips was gentle, a foray. As she opened for him, his hold tightened and he growled, a dam breaking loose, and then the gentleness of him was gone. Between one second and the next Amberley wasn't sure if she was kissing the man, or the Bear.

Tongue invaded her mouth, suddenly sharp teeth nipped at her lips. He kissed her expertly, a deliberate onslaught of dominant passion.

She gasped against his mouth, needing air, heart racing. Needing him. Her hands grabbed his shoulders, nails digging into thermal covered muscles. Hard flesh.

A sudden tap on the window and Amberley jerked, squeaking. Jayson pulled away slowly, eyes fixed on her face, eyes lightened to a deep amber glow. And then he glanced over her shoulder, face sliding into its cheerful public mien.

"Coming, Mrs. Montgomery."

Amberley twisted back into place in the seat, feeling the heat in her cheeks, and glanced at the frowning divorcee who held two mugs of steaming liquid. Amberley doubted one was for her. Oh, well. It was time word began to spread that Jayson Conroy belonged to her now.

***

Word spread fast. Amberley was stunned at the number of old high school girlfriends who came into the shop, curious and congratulatory.

"I heard Jayson Conroy staked a Claim," one female said, a member of his Clan Amberley recalled as being a grade behind her.

She boxed up the female's cupcakes. "Yes. We're courting."

"Gwenafar must be ecstatic. But- oh. Your Mom

doesn't like shifters, does she?"

And that was how most of the conversations went. Evidently Laticia's reputation preceded her. Amberley just bided her time. Mom hadn't said anything else about the courtship, hadn't even acknowledged that news was running like wildfire through their social circles.

The silence made Amberley very, very nervous.

"Don't worry about it," Jayson said, leaning on the counter as she closed shop a week later. "Gwenafar is handling things."

Amberley took off her apron, having finished the last of her cleanup, and thought about hiring a part time employee with all the new traffic coming in. Maybe a high school student who needed some experience on their resume.

"You don't know my mother very well. She's up to something, I know it."

He slapped her bottom as she passed. Amberley jumped, whirled, and glared at him. It wasn't like his touch was light as a feather.

He grinned. "It'll give us something to think about. And I've got a surprise for you tomorrow morning to help relax you."

"A surprise?"

"You'll see."

5

He took her to the local craft store for a baking class.

At first, Amberley refused to get out of the truck. "Are you insane?" she asked, voice hot.

Jayson stood next to her, passenger door open, reaching across her to unbuckle the seatbelt as she tried to tug it away from him. "You have to learn how to bake, Stormy," he said, oh so reasonable. "What happens if one day all the magic goes poof? We were going to use your income for the vacation and college funds."

"I- what?"

He grinned. "I'll pay the bills, you fund the entertainment and extras."

She stared at him, eyebrow raised. "Is that how your parents handled the budget?"

His expression darkened. "No. They're divorced."

She'd forgotten that. His parents were one of the rare shifter couples in town who had split. Amberley bit her lip. "I'm sorry."

He leaned forward, giving her a swift kiss. "Don't worry about it."

"Jayson, I can't walk into a baking class. I'm supposed to be able to bake already."

"We'll tell them it's for me to learn. Like you thought it would be one of those fun, girly couple's dates."

Amberley sighed. It wasn't like she could physically stop him from unbuckling the belt. She allowed him to lift her out of the truck, as well.

"This is just the worst idea ever, Jayson Conroy, but I'll do it for you."

He slung an arm around her shoulders and escorted her in. Several pairs of eyes turned towards them when they entered.

"Bringing him into the family business," Amberley said, making a half-hearted joke.

She warmed up as the lesson proceeded. Her batter didn't turn out any better than normal, but her decorations were flawless as usual. Jayson stared at her finished set of twelve.

"If I didn't know better... those look good enough to eat."

A passing woman heard him and laughed. "Such a tease, Jayson."

Amberley smiled weakly. "Wonderful sense of humor."

"I just don't understand it," he said as they drove away. "I watched you like a hawk. Your measurements were correct. You used the right ingredients. Well, you swapped almond for vanilla, but-"

"Not on purpose."

He waved a hand. "Still not a big deal. It could be

misconstrued as playing with flavors. Why the hell don't your recipes work?"

"I've thought about it. I think maybe my magic affects the chemistry of the baking process, and I have to use my magic to make it normal again."

He grunted. "That's as good a theory as any, I suppose." Jayson sighed. "But that means if your finger ever breaks-"

"I'd just hire an assistant baker. I was planning to anyway, when I have enough revenue to justify an employee. Another year and I can take on help."

"Maybe you should do catering, add an extra stream of income."

They pulled up to her house. "That's a good idea."

Once inside, she immediately tossed the box of cupcakes away. Jayson sat down at the kitchen table, laughing. She wrinkled her nose at him and opened the fridge.

"I made a pitcher of tea," she said, pleased. Some evenings she forgot to steep her leaves and since she didn't like the taste of plain water, she had to have the tea just to stay hydrated. She'd been certain she'd forgotten last night's batch, but things were so busy lately she must have brewed it on autopilot and just forgot.

"Better be sweet," her Bear said, leaning back on the legs of his chair. He patted his lap. "Come sit here, female. I have some etchings to show you."

Amberley snorted, taking two glasses out of the cabinet. "You are not funny."

But she obliged, settling in his lap and pouring the tea. She waited as he took a sip, grimaced, and set it down.

"That is definitely not sweet."

She raised her glass to her lips, smiling, and drained her glass before pouring a second. "You develop a taste for it. The sugar corrupts the natural flavor of the leaves, you Neanderthal."

"I am a Bear." He slid an arm around her waist, pulling her against his chest, his other hand delving into her hair. "A hungry Bear."

Jayson lowered his head, brushing lips along her cheek, trailing down to nuzzle her neck.

"What did you have a taste for?" she asked, breathless.

"Something spicy, and sweet."

He wasn't talking about food.

Clever fingers slid up her hips, delving underneath her shirt to cup her breasts. Amberley moaned low in her throat, shifting on his lap to straddle him, a fire beginning between her thighs. Sexual desire had always been a low, slow burn with her. She'd kissed a few men, even gotten as far as an open shirt. But she'd just never wanted anyone else, even though she'd tried. Tried to make her body feel something more than a casual sexual curiosity. But no matter how she tried, she was easily turned off or distracted.

But a moment later when her stomach clenched, it wasn't with desire. Amberley tore away from him, scrambling off Jayson's lap and backing away, a hand to her mouth.

"What am I doing?" her voice trembled. "I don't want this!" She'd held herself all these years, hadn't wasted her body on a man's disgusting lust, and now here she was letting a Bear put his hands all over her.

He rose slowly, eyes trained on her face. Eyes the color of mud, dirty and full of deceit.

"Stormy?" She hated that name. Hated that he disrespected her Coven lineage by giving her such a ridiculous moniker. Immature, classless. Not fit for a witch, a woman of good family.

"Go. Just go. I'm making a mistake, I don't know why-"

She whirled, needing to get away from him, stomach nauseous. Head pounding as if she'd had a hangover. Not that she knew what a hangover was like, but-

"Amberley."

Sharper now, his voice right behind her, following her as she fled the kitchen, trying to escape to the bedroom. Amberley whirled, glaring at him. Placed two hands on his chest and shoved.

Then recoiled; touching him hurt.

"Baby, something is wrong."

"I'm not your baby! Get away from me, just go!"

She was about to scream. Amberley clutched her head, moaning. "Thirsty," she whimpered.

"You just drank an entire glass of tea."

"Please, go. Why won't you leave?" She leaned against the wall, knees trembling, face shielded by her hands.

"Okay, baby, I'm leaving."

As she heard his steps lead him from the house, she slid down the wall, and burst into tears.

***

She hadn't sensed his rage.

Jayson jerked as the sound of her crying reached him, even as he got into his truck. He sat in the seat a minute, eyes closed, taking a deep breath. His hands wrapped around the steering wheel, hard enough he feared he'd break it.

That bitch.

No choice but to leave Amberley, she wasn't in any state to listen to him. He'd seen the change in her eyes, smelled the strange scent wafting from her skin. The scent that matched the herbal tea she tried to serve him.

Wanted to go to his female, comfort her. But Jayson knew unless Laticia fixed whatever she'd done to that tea, Amberley wouldn't be able to hear him. He could only hope Stormy wouldn't hurt herself while he was gone, but would cry herself to sleep. Or better yet, puke up the tea.

He told himself, as he drove the few blocks to Laticia Levinson's home, that he couldn't kill his future mother-in-law. What kind of female poisoned her own daughter? He wondered if the tea had been meant for him, for Amberley, or for them both.

And he wondered why Laticia thought he was fucking stupid.

He pulled up outside the house, shut off the truck and strode up the walkway, banging on the front door. Fangs itched; Bear rumbled, restless. Wanting a fight.

The door opened, a statuesque woman with burnished brown skin staring at him through a screen.

"How can I help you?" she asked.

Jayson smiled, showing his fangs, and placed a hand on the door frame, leaning forward.

"I've known Amberley for eight years. I know how she smells, I know how she talks. I know what she says when she's angry. I don't know what the fuck you did to her, but you're going to undo it or I will be at your doorstep with more trouble than you and an entire Coven can handle."

Laticia stared at him, face impassive, and then sighed. "She drank the tea?"

The gall of the witch to just blithely admit to... he counted to ten. Started over several times until he could count, coherently, without thinking violent thoughts.

"Get back in your truck and drive away," she said. "I'll deal with my daughter."

The door slammed in his face.

Jayson stared at it.

Stared at it.

And roared.

***

Fortunately, the Sheriff was a Bear. The neighbors had called, rightfully concerned, and Mike arrived in record time because hell, if there was a rampaging Bear on the loose, the Clan didn't want humans anywhere near him. Jayson endured the blistering lecture and twenty-minute cool down in the back seat of a squad car, and promised not to yell at Laticia Levinson any more- even if she was trying to ruin his courtship. He wasn't the only male who'd ever had to endure reluctant parents not wanting to give away a darling female to some burly male with decidedly lascivious intentions.

"I have a hex with your name on it, Jayson Conroy," Laticia said from inside her house. "If you ever raise your voice to me again."

He said nothing, wincing when she slammed her door.

Mike snorted. "Way to start relations with the future in-law. Go home to your female- you'll have a lot of smoothing over to do, scaring her mother like that."

"That female wasn't scared for a second."

"Go!"

***

Amberley jerked, a hand on her shoulder. The movement made the contents of her stomach slosh around. She pressed a hand to her throbbing forehead, and threw up.

An exclamation of disgust. "It shouldn't have affected you like this."

She struggled to understand the words. Her mother helped her to her feet and to the bathroom to clean up. When she was done, she stumbled to her bedroom and managed to get into the bed.

"I'll take care of the hallway," Mother said from a distance.

Sometime later, a steaming mug of liquid was placed against her lips. "Drink it."

Amberley didn't want to drink anything. But the salty chicken scent reached her nose and suddenly she was ravenous.

"Chicken noodle soup," her mother said "The best counter to the brew I've ever come across."

She sipped for a while, and when her head was normal again and she could think, she rose from the bed and went into the living room where her mother sat, watching television.

"You brewed an anti-love potion."

Laticia glanced at her. "It would have worked if he had had some, too. I didn't think it would make you sick, though." She sighed. "Our bloodline is weak."

Amberley turned and went into the kitchen, sitting down at the table. The pitcher was empty, rinsed out and turned over onto the counter to dry. What could she do? Her mother had raised her, alone mostly. Done her best. She could be a cold, controlling... witch. But she'd worked her ass off to support Amberley over the years, especially during the times, like now, when her human father was gone on one of their many separations.

But something had to give. They couldn't keep going on like this.

"Drink some more soup," her mother said in the doorway. "And call me if you feel sick again."

Amberley stayed seated, and sipped more soup, listening to her mother's car pull off. She didn't have long to wait.

***

"They called the Sheriff on you?" she asked Jayson in disbelief.

He cradled her on the couch, grip tighter than normal.

"I was kind of angry, Stormy."

She sighed. "We can't murder my mother."

He grunted. "Everyone has in-law issues. My in-law

just happens to be a witch."

"Hedgewitch."

"Whatever."

Her cell rang and Amberley unwound from her Bear, grabbing it off the TV stand. "Oh, joy. It's Gwenafar. She must have heard." She pushed connect. "Hello?"

"Amberley, dear, how are you?"

"I'm fine. We're fine."

"That's good to hear. I have a little request for you. Rebekah is having a Solstice mating ceremony, and you know she's one of these modern girls. Not very traditional."

Amberley blinked. Jayson shrugged. It wasn't what either of them had expected to hear.

"Yes?"

"Well, if you're interested we'd like you to cater the wedding cake. Cupcakes, really, which is the non-traditional part."

"Oh! I'd be glad to. Can you fill out an order inquiry on my website? It goes into a spreadsheet so I can stay organized. And tell her there's no charge- a mating present."

"That's very sweet of you, dear-"

Amberley squeaked as Jayson nipped at her neck, hard.

"Is something wrong, Amberley?"

She cleared her throat, reaching around to pinch him. Hard. "No, not at all." He pinched her back. "Jayson!"

"Ahhhh…" Gwenafar's knowing voice sounded like a smirk. A self-satisfied smirk. "You must be busy. I'll let you get back to your company." Gwenafar paused. "Maybe a double Solstice ceremony, hmm?"

6

"You're supposed to be a guest," Rebekah said, pale eyes flickering in annoyance. "I don't know what Grams was thinking."

Amberley smiled at Rebekah. They hadn't been close friends in high school, being in different grades, but they'd done a few projects together. Though many students thought Rebekah was cold, troublesome and a little weird, Amberley had always thought her brisk, guarded but loyal and warm- once she trusted you.

"It's okay, it's like free advertising," Amberley said. "Now go- you need to get dressed and I'm going to get the dessert table setup."

Rebekah scurried away, face brightening with a combination of happy anticipation and bridal dread. Amberley smiled and returned to the building's small kitchen where trays of wrapped desserts were waiting. Another company was catering hot food and beverages, but Amberley oversaw the dessert table. Since she only produced cupcakes and a limited range of baked goods, she'd negotiated with Gwenafar for a budget to subcontract some local bakeries for a wider selection of treats.

A hand sneaked around Amberley as she began decorating cupcakes. She transported the treats unfrosted to avoid damage in the catering truck.

She slapped Jayson's hand. "Stop that. You wait your turn- and there will be plenty of leftovers to take home."

He kissed her neck. "True. I know the baker, so I can have all the cupcakes I want."

She leaned against his back, the Bear a rock steady wall behind her. An arm snaked around her waist, and a chin rested on her head for a moment.

"That's a lot of cupcakes, Stormy. Your finger must be tired."

"That's it." She couldn't have him alluding to her magic in front of the humans. She was walking a fine line as it was, both ethically and per food service laws. "You get out, go find a Bear and spike the punch bowl or something."

He snorted, but obeyed. "I'm far too old to spike the punch bowl," he said as he left. "I'll bribe a cub to do it."

She grinned when he left, not wanting to encourage his bad behavior to his face, and finished the decorations as she directed assistants to set up and decorate the table according to the planogram she'd provided.

And then it was time for the ceremony. Amberley took her place next to Jayson in the circle that would surround the couple. She squeezed his hand, in awe of how staff had transformed a plain, industrial studio set into a winter wonderland. It looked like a magazine wedding, and she knew they'd planned it on a budget and a tight deadline.

"Oh. Oh," Amberley breathed when Rebekah appeared. "She's beautiful. I never really saw it before."

They'd dressed the bride in deep maroon, embroidered with gold and black threads, and winking with tiny beads. The dress was obviously from the groom's culture, and made her look like a faraway princess, her long black hair draped over her shoulder. Blue eyes bright, lined mysteriously in kohl. Amberley glanced at the groom, a Bear she'd only met today. He had eyes just for Rebekah, and the intensity of his handsome, swarthy face made it obvious the two were a perfect pair.

Gwenafar had done it again, darnit.

"They look gorgeous," she murmured. "Gwenafar is congratulating herself."

Jayson's hand caressed her hair. "She does a mean job of matchmaking."

His lips barely moved, the words just for her ears. Her spine tingled, skin shivering with desire as his warm breath touched her ear.

"Later," he promised in a dark voice. A knowing voice.

The heat between them deepened. Over the last several days it had nearly spiraled out of control several times. It was always Jayson who held back.

"I want you to have a proper courtship," he'd said.

"Don't you think I should make the decision myself whether to jump your bones?"

He'd arched a brow, though his eyes remained stubborn. "Maybe I'm just holding out until you get hot and heavy just once to seal the deal."

As if he had to worry about that. They moved in rhythm, an easy familiar friendship between them that just fell into place, as if they'd been dating ages. The almost routine of the relationship was a comfort. It assured Amberley that once they settled into the boring daily grit of marriage, they could still be happy. That they were more than just a couple in the glow of a new relationship.

The party was underway as soon as the ceremony ended, the newly mated couple retiring to a quiet corner. Amberley dashed in and out of the kitchen, ensuring the dessert table remained replenished, neat and well attended. She watched as a teenage beauty walked too casually away from the beverage station, liquid dark eyes innocent.

Amberley's eyes narrowed and she looked for Jayson in the crowd. He was with a group of male Bears, laughing raucously and plowing through plates laden with food. He pretended he didn't feel her trying to capture his attention- any other time all she had to do was focus on him, and she had his attention immediately.

Amberley snorted, returning to her work when Rebekah waved a hand from across the room. A tall, lethal-looking woman stood next to her, a flowing navy blue skirt in swaths of sheer fabric and a tight top giving the illusion of femininity.

She looked like she had a few spells tucked under her bodice.

Amberley trotted over, eyeing the woman- who must be related to the groom- as she munched on one of Amberley's cupcakes.

"Is everything ok?"

"Everything is fine," Rebekah said. "The cupcakes taste great. My sister-in-law wanted to talk business."

Amberley relaxed. She'd been hoping for some referrals from a party this size. Out-of-town referrals were even better, because it expanded her reach.

"Let's go outside," the woman said. "I need some fresh air and we can talk there."

"Is Rebekah's mate your brother?" Amberley asked as they exited the building to the parking lot. Night had already fallen and a gentle brush of snowflakes drifted to the ground under the lampposts, twinkling in the air.

"Yeah, my older brother."

"They make a very handsome couple. I'm glad Rebekah is happy, she deserves it."

"We're very happy to have her as a sister. I'm Asiane." The woman inhaled. "And you smell like witch."

Amberley blinked. Bears. "Well... I'm a hedgewitch. Mostly human now."

"Hmm. I thought these cupcakes tasted a little too good to be true." Knowing eyes fixed on her face. "No one else knows, huh? Good for you."

"My magic is perfectly harmless," Amberley said with great dignity. "And I only use it to ensure the recipes act properly. Not to-"

Asiane waved a hand. "Yeah, yeah. As long as they aren't poison, I don't care. Rebekah suggested a Ladies' Night at my place- I run a club."

"You wanted cupcakes?" Amberley asked. "Does that mix well with alcohol?"

Asiane shrugged. "I guess we'll find out." The female smiled, arch. "Sugar, booze, naked males... what could go wrong?"

It sounded fun. "I wonder if Jayson would let me go?"

"The male you're with? Tell him to put a ring on it."

Amberley laughed, turning her head as the sound of wheels approaching grabbed her attention. Asiane followed her glance, unconcerned.

Amberley frowned. "Why would a catering van park

over here?" she asked as it pulled up close to them. "The kitchen is on the-"

"Fuck." Asiane grabbed her, nearly tossing Amberley. "Go, get my brother."

The back door of the white van opened and a Bear surged out, two human males jumping from the passenger side. Asiane met the attack, no time to shift. Amberley screamed as the Bear rose on hind legs, the human shoving Asiane into reach.

Her magic wasn't strong, and certainly wasn't offensive. But she ran towards the human, wishing for a second that she was from one of the Old Families and could simply focus pure power into something deadly. But all she could do was brew herbal spells and fix broken cupcake recipes, little bits of tattered energy to do silly things.

The human grabbed her by the arms and threw her towards the ground, out of his way. The sharp force of her head against the cement stunned her.

When her vision cleared, Rebekah was kneeling next to her, rage and fear in the newly mated woman's face.

"Amberley, what happened?"

"They took Asiane."

She'd heard the female's snarls, the sound of doors slamming and wheels screeching off. She should have gone to get help, but she'd been afraid to leave Asiane. Hadn't wanted to feel like a coward for fleeing. It hadn't mattered anyway- she'd been worse than useless. Amberley sat up, anger bubbling. Worse than useless.

"Tell me everything you saw," Rebekah's mate ordered, voice cold with intensity.

"Stormy!"

Rebekah was helping her to her feet as Jayson burst

through the door. Eyes black, face pale. He was at her side in an instant, body subtly pushing Daamin aside.

"I was in the kitchen- I heard screaming."

Less than a minute, maybe two since the van had driven away.

"White van, I thought it was a catering truck," Amberley said, leaning into Jayson's embrace but looking towards Daamin. "There was a Bear and two human males."

"Features?"

"Dark hair and eyes, brown skin. Like you- the same kind of facial structure."

She was uncomfortable a moment, not wanting to stereotype an ethnic group by admitting they all kind of looked similar to her. Amberley sighed, turning in Jayson's arms. Her sandy-haired, dark-eyed, pale-skinned male. His being white didn't bother her mother- no, Laticia's prejudice was against shifters. But it was still prejudice.

"I think I hit my head," she muttered against his chest. Her drifting thoughts were odd, considering a woman had just been kidnapped.

Jayson lifted her into his arms immediately, striding back into the building. Daamin and Rebekah were talking, an accented female voice joining the conversation. It wafted over her, the words not penetrating the dense headache centered in her forehead.

"We must go," she heard Daamin say. "I would advise you not let your female out of your sight for the next several weeks. My sister was taken by enemies. And now your female has seen their faces."

7

Jayson made her stay awake. Someone quietly took charge of the rest of the party, and with packing up her shop's supplies. Scrapes she hadn't been aware of until they began to sting, were cleaned and tended. Jayson ushered her into his truck, the heat blasting. He spoke with Gwenafar a few moments, Liam also present, grim-faced.

When he opened the driver side door and got in, he reached across the seat to take her hand and press a kiss on her palm. "You may have a concussion, and until we know whether or not you're safe, you need to be guarded at all times. We're going to take you to a hospital-"

"No. No hospitals." She grimaced. "I'm a witch, Jayson."

He paused. "Okay." All extra-human species disliked hospitals, afraid someone unscrupulous would take DNA samples. Things had happened in the past. "But you're coming home with me, Stormy, so I can keep you safe."

She thought it was a bit of an overreaction, but Bear males were like that. And it hurt her head to protest, especially since she was sleepy.

"Stay awake, baby," he said, turning on the air conditioner and blasting music. The cold air hit her in the face and she squealed. "I'm sorry, Stormy. I've got to keep you awake."

She grit her teeth and made her eyes stay open. After a stop for some hot gas station tea- terrible, but better than nothing and it gave her something to do- they were on the road again.

At home, instead of turning off the exit that led into town, he stayed on the now two-lane highway for several more miles before turning off onto an unpaved exit that led deeper into the woods lining the highway.

"You live in one of the forest neighborhoods?" she asked.

There were several Bear families in town that preferred to live away from the humans and had small houses spread out in clusters.

"Yes. I finished my house a few years ago."

"I remember." There had been talk during construction by several of the single women at Al's place. Speculation that since he was building a den, Jayson would be picking a mate and settling down soon. After he settled in but made no effort to move a female in with him, talk had died down.

They pulled up to a ranch style house. The front yard was just some cleared land, and there was a cement porch with an awning in front. A porch light was on, illuminating a dirt walkway.

No flowers, no landscaping. His porch furniture was a few folding lawn chairs and a thrift store-looking side table.

Oh, this wouldn't do. But she'd have to withhold judgement, and right now she didn't have the energy for more than a general sense of feminine disapproval anyway. He hopped out of the truck, at her side in a second, unbuckling her belt and lifting her out.

"I can probably walk," she said, leaning her head against his shoulder.

He kissed the top of her head. "Let me feel useful."

Jayson turned on the living room light once they were inside. He settled her onto a brown leather couch, stuffing warm colored throw pillows behind her, then retrieved a throw blanket in similar shades.

"There's no television in the bedroom," he said. "I thought we could sit up a while. I'll make some tea. I bought a tin of that loose-leaf stuff."

While he was gone, she fiddled with the remote, finding a baking championship on a food channel. He returned after a few moments, setting two mugs of hot tea on the wood and glass coffee table, then switched on a tall lamp and turned off the overhead lights.

He settled next to her on the couch, handing her the mug and two white pills. "Tylenol. Take it."

They watched television in comfortable silence for a while. A knock on the door and Meredith Conroy entered, Amberley's pink backpack in her hand.

"I brought you some clothes and items," the red-haired beauty said. "Brick taught me how to jimmy locks years ago- I hope you don't mind too much."

Amberley smiled weakly. It was such a small-town thing to do, and besides, she knew Meredith wasn't a thief and didn't strike her as being a snoop either.

"It's fine, thank you."

Meredith seemed relieved, and set the backpack next to the coffee table. "Good. If either of you need anything, call me. I have to go, Liam needs me to help with the trouble going down."

Amberley drew the blanket tighter around her when Meredith left. "Do you really think I might be in danger?"

He pulled her onto his lap. "I don't know, Stormy. But I'd rather be safe than sorry. A few days here with me won't be so bad, will it?"

No. Not bad at all.

***

The storm expected to hit began the next day. On top of worrying about the closing of her shop, and spending time poring over her finances to see if she was in the green enough to hire somebody, Amberley now had to stare out the window at the snow.

She hated snow. Cold, wet, a challenge to shovel through. The only good thing about snow was that it lent a beautiful backdrop to the Solstice holiday. Jayson tried to cheer her up that evening. A large box arrived and he let her do the honors of opening it.

"Prime One Day shipping," he said, sounding satisfied.

Amberley understood his self-satisfaction when the box revealed a selection of Solstice decorations. Candles of gold and white, a swath of silky cloth and dried evergreen boughs twined with silver. Twinkling silver stars to hang from… something.

"We don't have a tree," she said. It was one custom of her father's she'd always loved at this time of year. The tree. Usually decorated in silver tinsel and stars and set next to the mantle.

Jayson went to the front door and began pulling on his boots. "I'll go get you a tree. There are lots of trees right outside."

It was sweet, really. She could almost see his chest swell, the masculine desire to hunt something down and bring it home for the female. Amberley smiled, unpacking the decorations and beginning to plan for the living room when he left. She'd be sure to offer him lots of praise, and look suitably impressed when he dragged a tree home. She just hoped he recalled it couldn't be any taller than the height of the ceiling.

She settled down after an hour, and began to worry after two. Where was he?

After a dozen dark scenarios played in her mind, Amberley got into her boots and coat and went outside to look for him. The snow was coming down hard, already at her calves, and the wind gusted regularly, numbing her half-exposed face and freezing her legs through her jeans. She should have put on a pair of thermal leggings, but she hadn't been thinking.

When she heard growls and the crunch of heavy feet in snow, Amberley knew something was wrong.

***

He fought the enemy, the snow demon swiping at Jayson with fearsome claws. Ropy shoulders and elongated arms, it was a grotesque creature. All the more grotesque because it bore traces of Amberley's face.

His mate was somewhere in there, somewhere inside this red-eyed nightmare that had subsumed her. His ax lay several feet away, abandoned when she'd approached him with a bright smile and cup of steaming liquid. He'd chided her for coming out in the snow but welcomed the drink, about to escort her back into the house when her smile twisted into a snarl and she leaped at him.

He'd been forced into a shift to defend himself, had tried not to hurt her but after a while it became apparent the creature was trying to kill him. Keeping Laticia's trick in mind, he didn't know if the creature in front of him really was Amberley, or some strange witch's familiar made to look like his female.

It caught him with its claws, slicing ragged, bloody furrows that seeped through his fur.

A female's scream, what he thought was another trick, and then he saw her. The real Amberley, staring at him and the enemy with horror on her face. The distraction cost him. The creature leaped, taking advantage and Jayson rose onto hind legs to catch the attack, wrapping the creature in his powerful arms and tumbling them both to the ground, snapping at a sinewy white neck with his fangs.

Latin streamed over him, words sparking in the air. And then the creature was gone, evaporated in a spark of light and snowflakes. Amberley ran forward, throwing herself at him, heedless of claws and fangs. How did she even know it was him? When had she ever seen his Bear?

"It was just an illusion, Jayson. A child's trick we all learn the counter spell to before they even let us out of grade school."

The blood and pain was real. He began to shift, Amberley backing away to give him room. When he was done, he fell to his knees in the snow, the cold biting into his skin as blood seeped from his arms. The tatters of his clothing were somewhere.

She approached, wrapping an arm around his shoulder,

bumping herself underneath his bicep.

"Come on, let's get back to the house," she said. "You'll be disoriented until the illusion spell wears off. How in the world did she manage to do it?"

"If this is an illusion, how was I wounded?" he asked, voice a deep growl.

"Because your mind told you that you were wounded. That's why they are dangerous. And forbidden. My mother thinks I won't turn her into the Coven for this trick."

Anger seethed from her voice. With each step, his mind cleared and strength returned, rage accompanying the rapidly healing wounds. When they entered his house, Jayson turned to her, grabbing Amberley by the upper arms.

"I'm not going through this," he said.

She stepped back, face shuttering. "I understand. It's too much for any male to deal with. I'll go."

He swore at her, the only time he'd ever done so. And the last time, because he immediately felt like a piece of shit when she blinked several times, glancing away.

"No, damnit, that wasn't what I meant. I'm never letting you go." He yanked her against him, seizing her mouth in a dangerous kiss. A possessive kiss, body hardening. A sudden, fierce, nearly painful ache. "But we have to deal with her."

Amberley nodded, pulling away. Jayson wanted to howl in frustration. She continued to shield her eyes from him until he grabbed her chin and forced her to look at him. The grey eyes glowed burnished silver.

"Jayson- I'm not safe right now. I had to gather too much power, and I'm feeling a little... punch drunk. I need to get away before I do something we both regret."

8

Amberley knew he didn't understand the danger. His eyes gleamed at her, a glitter to the chocolate orbs that told her he had absolutely no care for his safety.

She'd run towards the sounds of an animal growling, thrashing in the woods. Only to see Jayson in Bear form fighting an invisible foe. A scream ripped from her throat, more from anger than fear. There was enough magic left in her blood that she could see the glimmering outline of the illusion, the magical signature of her mother's distinct aural swirl. It was the kind of spell that required a physical anchor, usually in the form of something ingestible. How her mother had gotten him to drink a potion, Amberley didn't know.

In her strength-fueled panic, she'd done something she'd only managed to pull off twice in her life, and only under duress. She accessed her own weak internal pool of power, drew on the life energy around her and pummeled through Laticia's illusion, shattering it into oblivion. Only in the aftermath all that energy had to go somewhere. She absorbed it, struggling not to either vomit or drop to her knees.

She felt drunk, unstable. It was still too close to the surface and he would be vulnerable to her influence until her reserves settled back down into their deep, still internal pool.

It didn't help that the power seized on her most ardent desire, attempted to act on her behalf. The tendrils of power reached out to Jayson, fueled by sexual desire. Her body reacted, the place between her thighs tingling, filling with need.

He inhaled, stepping towards her, as her scent changed. The muscles of his chest and shoulders clenched, thighs tensing. Her eyes traveled along the length of his taut, hardened body, lingering briefly on the erection he displayed, completely unabashed.

"No, Jayson," Amberley said, taking a step back. "I'm influencing you right now, you need to get away from me."

It was wrong, no better than some frat boy spiking a girl's drink and taking advantage. She'd be no better if she let him act on the heat rising between them.

Jayson laughed. "Little witch, you can't make me want you because I already do. And have- for years."

She knew he wanted her. But it didn't matter that, at this moment, her power was taking away his choice.

"It's not the same thing."

He grabbed her wrist, reeling her into him. He was still stronger than her, body hard where hers was soft and yielding. Skin scorching, shifter heat running through him like a human fever.

"Take advantage of me, Stormy. I promise I won't regret it in the morning."

He kissed her, the touch of his lips and tongue melting

through her reserve. Not that there had been much reserve in the first place.

"But you wanted to wait," she said, struggling to think. He'd wanted to wait so they could court.

He growled. "I'm done waiting. When we're mated, your mother can't play these games anymore."

She didn't bother to deny his conclusion, especially when his hands were busy all over her body, gripping the flesh of her behind and squeezing.

And her internal dam broke. The weeks of pent-up sensual desire and frustration overwhelmed her good intentions. She seized his neck, pulling his mouth back down to hers in a dark, rough, nearly combative kiss. His gripped her hair as she pressed herself into him, fingers digging into his chest.

He swore. "You have claws, female."

She looked at her hands. The nails had lengthened, thickened, taking on a pearly gray hue, a razor-sharp edge. Witches had other ways of defending themselves, too. It wasn't all spells and potions. Some ancestor, somewhere, had been more than human and more than magic user.

Amberley smiled. "Don't worry, I won't hurt you."

Jayson inhaled, hands sliding around her waist, tight. "Stormy, you can hurt me all you want."

Amberley pushed him onto the couch, straddling his lap, placing her still sharp nailed hands on his bare chest.

He ran his tongue around his teeth. "Are you sure you-"

"Shut up."

She seized his mouth in a kiss, grinding her open legs against his groin, reveling in the feel of him pulsing beneath her, strong hands gripping her waist and sliding under the band of her jeans to cup the flesh of her ass.

Too much cloth. She pushed away from him, bent over to unlace her boots, knowing he was getting an eyeful of her cleavage, and kicked off the boots. Then she stood, wiggling out of jeans and panties and tossing them over her shoulder.

"Oh, fuck me," Jayson said, voice hoarse as she whipped her flannel shirt over her head and unhooked her bra, dropping the last bit of clothing to the ground as if it were trash. It was a quick little striptease, but she wasn't in the mood for a slow tease. She wanted. Needed.

"That is the idea, Jayson Conroy."

She was still riding high on the energy of the counter spell. Amberley straddled him again, not minding that his eyes were glued to her breasts. His hands rose, squeezing her flesh. Her head tilted back, a moan escaping her throat. His hands felt so good on her skin, heated, the careful strength even in his pinky finger. She reached for him, wrapping her hand around his cock, the long, thick pulsing rod stiff at attention. Engorged, the head glistened with drips of moisture.

"Next time, I'll take you in my mouth," she said. "But for now…"

Dimly, she realized her sudden sexual aggressiveness was out of character. And then she dismissed the thought. Maybe it wasn't out of character. Maybe she was finally discovering her character.

She felt powerful, watching the expression of pain and pleasure slid across his face, the glitter of his eyes and snarl on his lips as he moved under her. Focused on her, wanting her.

"Lose control," she whispered. "I want you to lose

control."

Amberley positioned her hips over his cock and impaled herself. Pain threw a cold bucket of temporary sanity over the tidal wave riding her, but as her body adjusted, reason fled. She undulated her hips, learning the rhythm, responding to his cries even as she adjusted to bring him into contact with the newly discovered spot inside her body.

Jayson gripped her hips and began moving under her, increasing the pace and force of their union, nearly wresting control until she grabbed his hair, snarling at him.

He returned the snarl. "Don't tell me to lose control if you don't mean it," he said, voice guttural. Nearly inhuman- her sweet, quirky, laidback male transformed into something demanding, controlling.

Her eyes narrowed, then she shrugged, tossing her hair. Saying nothing, challenge written all over her face.

The she was on her back, Jayson pulling her hips halfway off the couch as he knelt in front of her, spreading her legs wide, a hand on either ankle as he plunged inside her.

She screamed, gripping the edge of the couch as he fucked her, strokes bringing Amberley to the edge of pleasure and hurling her over.

But he wasn't done.

"Again," he said, pulling her off the couch and onto the floor

Amberley knew instinctively what he wanted, arranging herself on her hands and knees, giving a brief grimace to the hardness of the floor under her, but then couldn't think at all as hands gripped her breasts, his hard cock plunging inside her.

He ground inside her, a hand sliding down her body to play with her clit. Amberley moaned, gasping for breath as her body revved, helpless beneath him.

Jayson leaned over her, whispered in her ear. "All night, Stormy. I'm going to do dirty things to you all night."

Her knees trembled, head limp on her neck. Jayson withdrew, pulling her to her feet and backing her against the nearest wall. He lifted and she wrapped her legs around his waist, clinging to his shoulders as he entered her again.

And again, and again, each stroke firing her core.

The second orgasm shivered through her and this time he stiffened, cock grinding inside as he filled her body.

He lowered his head, nuzzling her neck, teeth scraping at her skin. "Mine," he whispered.

And when he lifted his head again, glowing eyes meeting hers, he said, "Again."

She froze. No matter how many times, it would probably always feel new to her. "Are you sure you're up to it?" she asked, some devil of mischief prompting her to arch an eyebrow at him suggestively.

His jaw loosened for just moment. "Am I... female, I'll take payment for that sass in flesh."

Amberley giggled when he lunged at her, spending a delightful minute wrestling. He held back, of course- there was no way she would ever get the drop on him in a fight, unless he was blind, intoxicated, lying prone in a sickbed and all that jazz.

They ended up with Jayson lying on his back, Amberley straddling him again in what she suspected was rapidly becoming his favorite position. Strong hands kneaded her breasts as she rode him, thighs aching from the unaccustomed exercise, but she had eight years to make up for.

"Stormy," he said, voice a hoarse breath. "I'm cumming. Slow down."

Not likely. She reveled in the fact that she could make his body lose control. He was hers.

"I love you, you know," he said, a hand rising to tangle in her mussed, damp hair.

Amberley stilled, looking in his eyes. A piece of her heart tore in two and reformed into something new, and whole. The pink and gold threads between them snapped to attention with a nearly audible hum. And then he was inside her, his heart, his mind. A searing flash of Jayson's consciousness before it retreated, leaving her with just the subtle sense of his presence.

He reared up, an arm around her waist, eyes wide and paling to amber gold. Amberley clutched his shoulders, calm even as his fangs appeared, a low growl rumbling in his chest.

"My mate," he said. "I knew it. I knew you were for me."

When his hold tightened, and his mouth closed over hers, she didn't protest. When his lips trailed down her neck and his hips began surging against her again, the pleasure of another orgasm rippling inside her, she barely felt the prick of his teeth in her neck.

***

She woke early the next morning, the ache between her thighs unabated. Every inch of her body felt deliciously used. But her mouth tasted like ashes. Amberley took a deep breath, focusing on calming the sudden leap of her heart, and climbed out of his bed, glancing at Jayson as he woke.

He rolled over, eyes opening. "Are you hungry, baby?"

She pressed a hand to her stomach. No, she wasn't hungry. Not at all.

"Jayson…"

His eyes opened fully and he frowned at her. "What's wrong?"

Of course, he'd be able to hear the burgeoning distress in her voice. "Jayson, I think I bewitched you."

He rolled onto his back, and laughed. "Stormy, you can witch me any day. And twice on the weekends."

"It's not a joke! It's… not good magic. It's wrong. Men are called rapists for doing less."

Jayson sighed and sat up. His eyes were a normal brown now. No tinge of pink, no manic shifter glow.

"Amberley, whatever you think you did, I'm fully myself. Even if your magic affected me a little- do you think it will be the last time that happens? Unless you deliberately override my will, it's not the same thing. Did you want me?"

"Yes, of course."

He continued, eyes trained on her face, voice reasonable. "Did I forcefully overcome your maidenly objections with my overpowering manly will?"

"No! Are you insane? And who talks like that?" She stared at him, irritated. He wasn't taking this seriously.

Jayson grinned at her, rolling to his feet. "Get back in bed, Stormy. I'll make us an omelet. You'll feel better full."

9

Amberley wasn't convinced, and she didn't think Jayson was taking her seriously.

"Okay, Stormy, what do you want me to do?" he asked finally, visibly exasperated. "Whip you? I don't have any hairshirts lying around."

"You aren't funny. Or Catholic. Take me to see my mother."

"What? Have you lost your mind? She's the one who started this in the first place!"

Amberley folded her arms. "Doesn't matter. We're bonded now so there isn't anything she can do against us. My mother is a practical woman."

He tried to argue her down, but she didn't budge. He wasn't a witch. She didn't expect him to understand.

Jayson drove her through the snow into the part of town where Laticia lived. "We should be cooking a turkey right now," he said, disgusted. "Not asking your mother for advice on our love life."

Amberley paused in the act of opening the truck door once he'd pulled up. "Oh! It's Christmas Eve, isn't it?" She hadn't celebrated in the last few years since her father had separated from her mother, but the night always brought back memories of a happier time in her small family. Amberley leaned across the seat to kiss Jayson's frowning mouth. "You know what, as soon as we get home, let's whip up a nice, big, Christmas Eve dinner. The grocery stores are still open. Not even the blizzard would shut them down tonight." Too much money to be had with last minute shopping.

Jayson sighed, leaning into her kiss, a hand on her cheek. "Hurry up, Stormy. This isn't my idea of a grand ole time."

She rolled her eyes and climbed out, running up the salted walkway and banging on the front door.

Her mother answered a minute later. "Amberley."

She pushed inside, shutting the door behind her with a sharp slam, and faced her mother. Despite what Jayson might think, she was pissed, and was going to have it out with Laticia right now- but Jayson didn't need to know of any discord between the females. His dealings with her mother were going to be hard enough without her asking him to absorb the residual tension of her own strained mother-daughter relationship.

Laticia took a long look at Amberley's face and snorted, folding her arms. She was in a deep purple velour robe, braids loose over her shoulders.

"What you did to Jayson was wrong, Mother. Shitty, and wrong. He could have been hurt."

Laticia turned on her heels and went into the kitchen. Amberley following behind her.

"Don't cuss in my house," the older woman said, voice

short. "That's him sitting outside? Evidently, none worse for the wear."

"No thanks to you! You're going to have to accept him, Mom. We're matebonded now."

Laticia set cast iron pot of tea on the kitchen table. "That is a shame. I'd hoped for so much better for you than a shifter handyman."

"Better than a man who loves and respects me? And he's an entrepreneur, self-supporting and even built his own house. A man who works like that will never let a family go hungry." Her throat closed. "And because we're bonded, he'll never leave, mother. Even if our cubs don't shift."

Laticia sipped her tea. "Has your father called you?"

"No."

"You're an adult, Amberley. You don't need him."

"No, I don't. I love him, and I love you. But I don't need either of you." Amberley placed her hands on the table, leaning forward. "If you can't accept the mate I've chosen, then I'll have to walk away, Ma. When we have cubs, that will be more important than anything else, that they have a stable, loving, two-parent home. I want them to know their grandparents, but not if that means conflict."

"Cubs." Laticia placed her teacup on the table with an audible blink. "Unbelievable. And if you think I'm allowing that man to raise my grandchildren without my influence, you're both dead wrong."

Something inside Amberley relaxed. It was as close to an apology she would get from her mother. The closest to open acceptance Laticia would offer.

Amberley sat back in her seat, and exhaled. "There's

something else."

Laticia's eyes narrowed. "What?"

"I think I bewitched Jayson."

Her mother stared at her, expression blank. Amberley returned the stare with significantly more expression, irritation rising.

"And?" Laticia prompted.

"Well, considering recent events you might not think it's a big deal, but I'm bothered by the fact that I coerced him into sex with me!"

Mother snorted, pouring herself another cup of tea. "Have some tea, and relax a bit, dear. The virgin histrionics are giving me vapors."

"This is serious," she said through gritted teeth. "Or is the whole reason we left the Coven not to avoid the darkening of our magic?"

"That was one reason, and hardly the most important." Her mother rolled her eyes, an expression she rarely indulged in, considering it unrefined. "Really, Amberley, that shifter has been chasing after you for eight years and you think you coerced him? You don't understand how the unfocused power works. It's not like in a spell, where you can make it do something that isn't natural. When you just tap the raw magic, it can only act on what is already there. Unless you're telling me you brewed a love potion? No? Then what is the problem?"

"The problem is that I feel like I did something wrong," Amberley said, voice quiet. "And instead of trying to tell me it's all good, why don't you try helping me?"

Laticia rose with a sigh. "Fine. We'll do a cleansing spell. If only it would cleanse you of the miasma of your matebond."

"Not likely."

"One can hope."

***

What the hell was taking so long? He stared out the window, fingers tapping on the steering wheel. Kurt Cobain came on and it distracted him for a minute, but then it was back to waiting, and flipping through the radio stations trying to find something other than a Christmas carol to listen to. He grimaced. Not that he didn't like Christmas carols in moderation, but by this time of the year he was always thoroughly sick of them.

What were they talking about in there? Females. He didn't hear any shouting, or anything breaking. No weird herbal scents and so far everything around him looked normal. He wouldn't put it past Laticia to try another trick just for the hell of it, but he was reasonably certain she wouldn't hurt Amberley. Under the dour expression and haughty demeanor, was a female as fierce over her cub as any Bear. Her methods of expressing her protectiveness were just a little skewed.

He had a strong, strong suspicion that Amberley's family was from a dark Coven. She was a sweet girl on a normal day, but he'd known her too long. Piss her off and... things... had a way of happening. That's why the whole town made sure Amberley and her mother stayed happy. History had already proved the best way to deal with a witch was with sugar, and not spice. Persecution, running them out of town... it never worked for long. He'd have to have a long talk with Stormy, though. She was hurting herself, denying a side of her nature that she needed for balance, to be whole. Nothing good ever came out of hiding away bits of yourself- they had a way of appearing unexpectedly, and in annoyingly violent circumstances.

"Come on, Stormy, kiss Mama Witch and let's go home," he said.

Damnit. Might as well take a nap. Leaning his seat back a few more inches, he prepared to settle in and rest up so he'd have plenty of strength to please his mate that evening, when a painful jerk in their bond warned him. He was out of the truck and up the walkway in a handful of seconds.

Goddamnit.

***

Mother brought down the wooden containers of herbs. Amberley wrinkled her nose at the strong smell of cloves, garlic and mint, but proceeded into the living room to clear away furniture and draw a simple circle. They weren't performing high Magick- their bloodline was far too weak for the powerful spells. No, hedgewitches had to do with simple herbal concentrations, a smidgen of raw power and the strength of meditation and aural auditing techniques.

She waited until her mother entered the circle with a glass decanter of tea, before closing it. They settled cross-legged, because trying to perform a ritual on one's knees was just silly. Amberley began the chant, Laticia joining in as she poured a cup of tea and handed it to Amberley.

She downed it in one gulp, knowing from experience that it was better to just get it over with, and controlled her gag reflex, feeling her mother's slight smirk.

And then she sank into the trance, her own words falling silent as Laticia began speaking.

"Tell me the stain upon your soul."

She heard the ritual question from a distance. Guilt welled, along with pain for using her magic in a way they'd vowed never to do. To coerce, for personal gain. They'd fled their ancestral home to avoid going Dark. But maybe it was in her blood.

Amberley confessed, blinking back tears. Her stomach roiled.

"Tell me the stain upon your soul."

But it was more than just turning her own lust on Jayson. It was the questionable way she used magic to run her business. She cheated, utilizing power to give her a talent she wouldn't otherwise have. To provide income she wouldn't otherwise be able to provide. Her head began to pound, guilt and negative energy seeping from her pores in acrid sweat.

And a third time. "Tell me the stain upon your soul."

The worst stain, the stain of cowardice. Of denying love. She'd loved Jayson for years, but she'd allowed the darkness of her own hidden insecurities keep her away from him, from a union that was meant to be. How many children had not been born, how much good had never come to pass because of her fear and insecurity?

"Be cleansed, and suffer the Dark no more."

The pain, the guilt, the hidden suffering was released, a bloody, blackened kernel she tore from her aura and flung away. Laticia reached out, caught it in her hand and destroyed it.

Amberley vomited the tea, pain rippling through her. A stinging headache and twisting in her gut as well as the remnants of emotional and psychic pain. She moaned, curling onto her side, knowing she could only wait it out. It was part of the process, to endure the cleanse without fighting it.

And then a Bear roared.

10

She insisted on making dinner.

"Stormy, we're fine with tuna sandwiches or something. You don't have to cook."

He argued all the way to the store. It had taken several minutes to calm him down, convince him that her mother hadn't been trying to poison her or work any arcane Dark magic. Another several minutes to get her small family to agree to sit down and eat a meal together. And several more minutes in the bathroom vomiting the rest of the tea as quietly as she could, listening to her mate pace outside the door.

Amberley turned, nearly swinging the shopping cart into him as it whipped around with her. He grabbed it at the last second, returning her glare.

"I'm making holiday dinner," she said, voice rising. "And my mother is going to eat with us, and there will be no more fighting!"

A few people glanced her way, sympathetic mothers who fully understood the stress of cooking for extended family who didn't always get along.

"Okay, okay, baby, don't yell." He released the cart, sidling away. "Why don't I go grab a pumpkin pie?"

Her eyes widened. "Are you kidding me? Processed pumpkin pie? I'm a baker. There's no way in-"

"Amberley."

She shut her mouth as the harried, slightly henpecked mate altered into a fully alpha male Bear, eyes hardening.

"You are not feeling well. You will allow me to get a pie, so you aren't on your feet any longer than necessary. And when we get home, you will sit at the table, and I'll help you with the meal prep. And I won't tolerate any more arguments from you or we're going to McDonald's."

Her mouth gaped, outrage strangling her breath.

"Sounds like a final offer, honey," a woman muttered, passing by.

Amberley took a deep breath, smoothed her hair over her shoulder, and sniffed. "Why don't you grab one of those pumpkin pies from the bakery? That way we don't have to wait on dessert."

"That's a good idea, Stormy."

She pushed the cart away. "I'll be in the dairy section."

They loaded up the cart and drove home, pulling up behind her mother's car. Laticia exited the driver's side as Amberley and Jayson climbed out, Jayson snarling at her as she tried to grab some bags from the back seat.

"Get inside, Stormy," he said. "I'll bring in the bags. Go boil water or something."

She let him get away with that because she understood

he was feeling a little extra snarly, and because he needed to feel useful anyway.

"Mother," she greeted. "I'm glad you decided to come."

Amberley unlocked the front door, stepping aside so Laticia could enter. Her mother slipped her boots off at the entrance, handing her coat to Amberley.

"I brought some tea," Laticia said as Jayson entered the living room, arms full of plastic sacks.

He stopped dead, head swiveling towards the older female. Laticia smiled at him, the curl of her lips slightly malicious.

"You have a lovely home," her mother said. "Such rustic charm. Amberley, how wonderful for you to have a.... blank slate to work with."

Amberley sighed, approaching her mate. She placed a hand on his chest and waited until she had his attention, then rose on her toes to place a kiss on his mouth.

"I'm feeling a little faint," she said. "Can you help me with the vegetables?"

Distracted, he seemed to forget about her mother and instead ushered her into the kitchen and made her sit down, setting bags on the floor and grabbing a cutting board and knife to place in front of her.

Laticia strolled in and shooed him away. "Go put some logs in the fire, I'll help in here."

His eyes narrowed. "No tea. Just don't go near anything liquid, period. Or seasonings. In fact-"

Her mother waved a hand. "That's all past now. If you want to help, you can boil the elbow pasta. Not even a Bear can get macaroni wrong."

The meal went surprisingly well, especially once they'd managed to get Jayson to turn his back long enough to add a bit of 'fairy dust' to speed the turkey along. Amberley secretly admitted the store-bought pie was a good idea. Even with her mother's help and Jayson hovering over her, she was tired by the time everything was done. Her mate watched her like a hawk as they ate, making sure Amberley tucked into her plate before attacking his own.

Mother eyed him. "I can see the grocery bill is going to be high. Especially once the children are older."

Amberley slanted a glance at her mother. Laticia was behaving rather well, but she knew better. It would take her mother time to get used to a shifter son-in-law.

***

Gwenafar called the next day as Amberley was shredding leftover turkey to make sandwiches.

"So will we be having a New Year's Day mating ceremony? I just happen to know someone who owns a party hall with a space available- a last minute cancellation, you know. It would be doing my friend a favor."

Jayson snorted, leaning against the counter. "Great timing."

Amberley met her mate's eyes. They were amused, rather than irritated, the warmth washing through their tender new bond.

"I think I have a dress I can wear," she said, voice soft.

Jayson leered. "I'd rather you didn't wear a dress at all."

"Well, since we're all in agreement," Gwenafar said, voice dry. "I'll text you the information. Tell your mother to behave, Amberley. Never mind- I'll tell her myself."

Amberley winced as she disconnected the call. "I'm glad I don't have to witness that conversation."

The hall fell through, oddly enough, so Gwenafar got her outdoor winter ceremony. On New Year's Day the Clan gathered in front of Jayson- and now Amberley's- home. Somehow the males managed to build a fire pit in record time, so they had a roaring bonfire- even though shifters didn't really need it. Because there was much furniture in the living room anyway, they set it up with long tables laden with food. Potluck style because of the short notice. Amberley and Laticia baked all evening, so the dessert table did her shop credit. But everyone else contributed a savory dish to the spread, and Alphonso made sure they were well stocked with a selection of booze. The good kind, too.

Amberley wore deep blue velvet, and a black cape edged in lace over the dress for extra warmth. Her mother interspersed silver beads and semi-precious stones in her hair, and refused to tell Amberley what spell the tiny stones were anchoring.

"You want cubs who can shift, don't you?" Laticia demanded when Amberley nagged her mother for the fifth time.

Gwenafar, perched on the bed ostensibly to make sure the bride didn't get cold feet, stared at Laticia, eye narrowing.

"You have magic that will ensure shifters?" the Bear demanded.

Laticia snorted. "Certainly not. If I did, I would have extracted a dear price from you long ago. I have magic that will... lean things in that favor. But only lean."

"We'll talk. I'll take a lean over nothing." Gwenafar seemed pet. "You should have said something years ago."

"No, I shouldn't have. It isn't wise to influence these things too often."

Amberley could tell Gwenafar wanted to argue, but chose to save it for another day.

The ceremony was blessedly brief- Amberley didn't enjoy being the center of so many pairs of eyes. And besides, she felt married anyway. A matebond was unbreakable... the ceremonies were mainly for the benefit of the unmated shifters in a Clan, a public confirmation that the couple was now off the shelf.

Rebekah and Daamin came, surprising Amberley. "Is there any word on Asiane?" she asked her new Clan mate.

Rebekah tensed. "Daamin has some contacts back in his homeland."

Amberley's eyes widened. "That's where she is? Brick, what's going on?"

"I don't know all of it, but it's Daamin's Clan business. At least you have an all clear."

Daamin had spoken with Jayson several days ago, and after the conversation Jayson informed Amberley that she was safe. They'd take the initial precautions just to be sure, but it was now apparent the Clan responsible for kidnapping Asiane wasn't interested in Amberley- she'd just been a bystander.

"If there's anything I can do... I'm not a strong witch, but if I can help, I will."

Rebekah squeezed her hand, Daamin approaching. "Thank you," the darker male said, accented words soft. "But I wouldn't put you in any danger."

"You wanted allies," Rebekah said to her mate.

"Warriors. Males. I don't take females to war."

"Asiane-"

"No, Rebekah."

Rebekah inhaled. "Fine."

"Will they be okay?" Amberley asked Jayson later.

"They're mates. And the Clan will help."

That evening they sat in front of the remnants of the bonfire, Amberley snuggling against her shifter husband for warmth, a blanket wrapped around them both for good measure.

"Do you wish it had been fancier?" he asked.

She peered up at his face, the bones sharp in the firelight. For a moment, he looked like a Slavic demi-god. Or demon. But definitely hot. She giggled.

"No, any fancier and it would have been stuffy."

He leered down at her. "You sound drunk. Can I take advantage of you? Maybe knock you up?"

She slid an arm around his neck, grinning when he surged to his feet with her in his arms. "Just as long as it's in a warm bed."

"Tonight, we mate. Tomorrow- we talk about fairy dust andcupcakes."

Claim your free romance here: smarturl.it/HowlList

Connect with Emma on Facebook at:
www.facebook.com/EmmaAlisyn

WANT MOAR?

CHECK OUT EMMA'S OTHER TITLES:

(Betcha can't read just one.)

CLAN CONROY BEARS

Liam's Bride

Alphonso's Baby

Norelle's Bear

What A Bear Wants

A Mate for the Bear

THE ROYAL BEARS

Bear Prince

Bear Princess

Bear Queen

MATES OF THE FAE

Fae Spark

Fae Wolf

ABOUT EMMA

Emma Alisyn writes paranormal romance because teaching high school biology wasn't like how it is on television. Her lions, tigers, and bears will most interest readers who like their alphas strong, protective and smokin' hot; their heroines feisty, brainy and bootilicious; and their stories with lots of chemistry, tension and plenty of tender moments. Stay up to date with new releases and get

Connect with Emma at:

www.emmaalisyn.com

http://facebook.com/emmaalisyn

Printed in Great Britain
by Amazon